EMPLOYEE 6 IS 54

EMPLOYEE 6 IS 54

By Nancy Branka

ISBN-13: 978-1-7377211-0-9

Cover design by Daniel Payne

For information, please visit: nancybranka.com or startupdecoder.com

*For my favorite intergenerational startup team,
Joe, Andy and Alex*

Contents

CHAPTER 1

J illian steadied her hand to touch the send arrow on her text: *I'm on the train to meet Desmond Hensley for coffee. I'm old enough to be his mother. #butIneedthejob*

Christian, her 28-year-old son, would no doubt text back a laughing emoji. But Jillian was only partly joking.

Christian was responsible for the meeting. Desmond Hensley had pitched Christian's VC firm for funding. While they decided not to back the company, Christian thought Sojourner might be an interesting fit for his mother. Still, Jillian thought it a little ridiculous that she was meeting with a startup founder about a job.

The day Christian told her about Sojourner, she'd gone straight to its website and clicked on Our Team. As expected, it was a small company. Christian said they were early-stage, but she wondered how they could do much business with—she stopped to count—five people. All guys. Variations on facial hair. Smart-looking. Hip. She read the CEO's mini-bio: Stanford MBA, previously with Boston Consulting Group, loves cigars, collects swords, and roasts his own coffee. The trend towards quirky bios annoyed her. Swords, really? And why does anyone roast their own coffee? In any case, at this point, she was in no position *not* to reach out. In fact, she was getting a little desperate.

One month prior Jillian had resigned from her role as sales director at Westbrook Hotels, where she'd worked for 30 (could it be?) years. She'd taken a stand against the new compensation structure upper management had just imposed on hourly workers. Some catering staffers were commuting two hours each way to make ends meet, sometimes working two jobs. And now to strip away their benefits? Her resignation was an indignant move. She'd stood up for what was right. But now she was out of a job. At 54. That, it turned out, was a problem.

A few years ago she'd taken her college graduation year off her LinkedIn profile, and more recently, she'd managed to make the date she started at Westbrook to be fuzzy. Last year she had migrated her personal email from hotmail to gmail, after she'd seen a cartoon in the New Yorker about hotmail for grandmas. In the last week, this vague discomfort had deepened.

Now since becoming unemployed, Jillian had been forcing herself to spend three hours each day on LinkedIn, Indeed and Glassdoor, making connections and applying for jobs for which she was, generally, overqualified. To date, she'd applied for 49 positions and had only landed a single interview. A phone interview. With a suburban hotel general manager, a man named Cody Joseph. (She noticed she pronounced his name mockingly in her head.)

Before they were too far into the interview, Cody Joseph asked what she made at Westbrook. Jillian paused. She knew any role in his organization would mean a pay cut for her, since over the years she'd worked herself into a very comfortable pay grade. But she was willing to do it. Yes, she and Scott had saved responsibly over the years in retirement funds, but she'd need some sort of income—even if not at the level of her Westbrook salary—to carry them through to social security. Scott had been generous not to mention this explicitly, but she knew the reality of it. Which was at the core of her fear that she'd never earn another dollar.

Of course, Cody Joseph didn't know she expected a pay cut and he probably assumed he couldn't afford her. Someone had told her that by state law employers can't ask candidates about the salary history. Should she tell him this and risk coming off as hiding something or seeming legalistic? Instead, she simply turned it back on him: "Are you able to tell me the salary range for the role?" Cody Joseph changed the subject, averting the problem—for both of them. He knew what he was doing. However, no job offer was forthcoming from Mr. Cody Joseph. And at this point, Jillian had come to not even expect a letter of rejection. To be ignored was to be rejected.

So now Jillian had resorted to attacking the second tier of opportunities—roles that were not an obvious fit. Her cover letters were attempts to connect the dots and explain why her experience at Westbrook Hotels was actually a brilliant match for whatever the obtuse opportunity. This crafting was probably a waste of effort: she knew companies use AI to scan resumes, and most are discarded before a human even sees them. She was not willing, though, to stoop so low as to stuff her resume with keywords, to trick the AI. Damn robots.

Thus, Jillian had fallen to filling afternoons with long naps and aimless scrolling on Facebook. So a coffee meeting with a startup founder was, at best, an exciting opportunity, and at worst, an excuse to get dressed and out of the house. Yes, she was surprised—shocked even—when Desmond Hensley had responded to her email. But she'd take it.

He had suggested they meet at Brew, around the corner from the Sojourner offices. This was a relief. The man was obviously a coffee snob, and she couldn't afford a misstep by suggesting Starbucks. Not that his expertise made him superior, she told herself. She was a tea drinker. Chances were he didn't know an oolong from a white tea leaf.

Jillian had dressed carefully that morning, unsure what was appropriate in the startup world. After staring into her closet for too long, she had finally pulled out dark jeans, boots and a black sweater. She dug through her scarf collection and picked out the black and turquoise paisley shawl she'd bought in India. Once dressed, she sized up the look in the mirror. *Not bad. This says, "I can be hip, too,"* she thought. She corrected herself, *"Hip-ish."*

Two hours later Jillian pulled open the door at Brew and stepped inside, met with the comforting aroma of coffee. She straightened her shoulders and tugged at her sleeve, then scanned the faces in line to order. Even from across the room, Desmond was instantly recognizable from the website photo—tall and lanky, dark cropped hair with just a touch of premature gray, a face that was soft and kind despite the gaunt drawn cheeks. The type who played a weekly pickup game of basketball. His jeans and button-down were finely tailored, clearly not Gap grade. Jillian thought he resembled her favorite of Christian's college roommates. Any fear she had melted away as she approached him in line. "Desmond?"

He extended his hand and smiled. "Jillian." The ensuing bit of small talk came easily—BART, the unseasonably warm day, and Christian.

"Listen, what can I get you to drink?" Desmond asked.

"Green tea, the smallest size, please. I'll get us a table."

One had just opened up by the window, a stream of sunlight cutting a bright swath across the tabletop. Settling and shoving her bag underneath, she took a few deep breaths. *Just exploration. This isn't about getting a job. It is simply making a new connection. It's all about talking to as many people as possible.* The voice in her head had a script.

Several minutes later he approached slowly, careful not to slosh her tea, which had been overfilled. He placed her cup gingerly on the table. Setting his own down and then sliding into the chair, he bent over the coffee and sniffed as if were an expensive Cabernet.

Desmond was a comfortable conversationalist, asking her about where she lived and where she grew up, the details about her family, and how she got into hospitality. Once he approached the subject of Sojourner he became a little more polished.

Sojourner, he explained, matched a hotel's most loyal customers with opportunities to engage in short community service projects right on the hotel premises during their stay. It was a win all the way around: the hotel could offer a unique experience to the guest, the guest could get to know another side of the city and feel good about offering an hour of time in service, and the nonprofit could enlist the support of new patrons. Sojourner facilitated all this through a web app.

What Desmond described didn't go much past what was on the website, though she appreciated the overview. "You are probably wondering about the business model," he added.

She nodded, feigning intrigue, even though Christian already told her about Sojourner's structure. Companies were willing to pay a marketing fee for the service for their loyalty program members, he explained, and eventually Sojourner hoped to offer corporations "subscriptions" for their business traveler employees. What Desmond described matched Christian's explanation exactly, which was a point in Desmond's favor. She'd learned a long time ago to watch for information matches, a double check on truth.

"How likely do you think it will be to enroll hotels in the program?" she asked. "Since that's where your revenue is coming from."

"My goal is to convert 90 percent of our target group. Of course, we are choosing those targets very carefully. From my perspective, it's a no brainer for them to sign up."

"Right…from your perspective." She knew that from a hotelier's perspective it wasn't such a no-brainer. "And if reality turns out to be more like 10 percent?" she asked.

"Then we either tweak the model, we do a major pivot, or we go out of business." He let that sink in as she took a sip of tea, but he was still smiling—an odd dissonance.

They discussed this a little more, Desmond eager for her insights into the hospitality business. Finally, he sat back in his chair. "Do you have any questions for me?"

Thank goodness Christian had coached her on this. He said she'd need to suss out the viability of the company. And its culture—anything dysfunctional. Early-stage startups can easily go off the rails, he'd told her.

She worried her questions may insult Desmond, so only asked a couple that Christian suggested about how financially sound the company was and growth plans for the team. His upbeat answers satisfied her, relieved her.

His face grew serious, as he looked her in the eye.

"Listen, it was great to have the conversation with you, and perhaps I could follow up on the phone? I don't want to jump the gun here, but I think your experience may be a good fit for our team."

As they stood and shook hands, her smile was as wide as it had been in weeks.

Maybe, just maybe, this could turn into something.

Three hours later, though, the rush of exhilaration of the early-afternoon coffee meeting had completely dissipated while she ran a few errands. The reality of her situation once again weighed on her like a backpack filled with textbooks. Really, what were the chances she'd get hired at Sojourner, despite happy coffee talk?

For now, though, she'd need to put on her cheerful face. She was walking to Zuni Cafe to meet Scott and Christian. When she'd kissed Scott goodbye that morning, he'd suggested they meet there for a dinner to celebrate her "new adventures." *That, of course, was presumptive*, Jillian grumbled to herself as she recalled the moment.

Early to the restaurant, she ducked into the restroom immediately inside the door where it was quiet. There she applied a fresh smear of lipstick and smoothed her shoulder-length hair, then stepped back from the mirror for a more favorable view. Sometimes she saw a stranger looking back at her, someone so different from the way she felt inside. Friends commented that she looked a decade younger than she was—but those were usually the ones who themselves were younger. She ran her hand through her hair again. Last year she'd sought a well recommended colorist to add highlights to her natural brown, a half-hearted effort to mask the gray roots that inched in every month. Maybe it was time to stop the madness of coloring it, let it go gray. Wouldn't that be freeing? *Oh god, I'm in the job market now—no way can I do that with gray hair.* She sighed and straightened herself, revising her body language in the mirror.

Shoulders back and chin up, she went into the restaurant and approached the maître d', following him through the buzzing restaurant to an empty table tucked in the back.

Jillian had always loved Zuni Cafe's iconic San Francisco vibe, which to her meant great light from an abundance of windows and an almost rustic, lofted space, along with California comfort food and the barely perceptible smoky smell of a wood-fired oven. The room was filled with a convivial mix of attorneys, investment bankers, and pre-opera diners. Just as she stashed her bag under the table, she heard his voice: "There she is, the brave and courageous Jillian Johnson." God, how she loved that voice.

Straightening, she stood and laughed. "Right, the *still unemployed* Jillian Johnson."

Scott pulled her close and held her there for a moment. "I have a good feeling about this," he whispered in her ear, followed by a kiss on the cheek.

Her sigh was more "that's a joke," than "thank you."

She met his eyes and her mood lifted, even if just a millimeter. After more than thirty years of marriage, she still marveled that she was able to land a man this handsome. At six-foot-three, he still carried himself as an athlete, and the gray in his longish hair had only mellowed the snowboarder-blond to a dusty golden. Best of all, he had no idea how good looking he was. Today he was wearing dark jeans and a heather gray hooded sweater. What worked for his young customers at the board shop somehow managed to look quite natural on Scott, too.

When Jillian and Scott met, she was a few years out of college and already working at Westbrook, a solid corporate job. Scott worked in the exact opposite of a corporate job: snowboarding. It was an unlikely profession with a distinct rebel culture. A hotdog rider from early in the sport, he had dropped out of community college and competed every weekend. For several years, sponsors had flown him to New Zealand and South America after the snow melted at Tahoe. But an ankle injury sidelined him early the year he met Jillian. Somehow their different backgrounds clicked on the first date, and he never quite regained that vagabond lifestyle, instead settling in Berkeley--and settling in as Jillian's steady boyfriend. Two years later they married. Two years after that, he opened On the Board, selling snowboards and skateboards to kids who were just like him.

Christian arrived at the table only a few minutes later and offered similar congratulations. This time she was able to relax and take in his optimism. She didn't want to discourage her own child from thinking positively about her. Besides, his well-educated opinion mattered to her, with a Stanford MBA recently added to his resume.

Christian was nattily dressed in VC casual: crisp shirt, dark jeans and a Patagonia down jacket. "This place is almost cool, it's so old-fashioned," he said, draping the jacket over the chair back.

"Old fashioned? You're kidding. It's the epitome of dining in San Francisco," Jillian said, turning to Scott for affirmation.

Scott nodded in agreement, his expression serious, like this was not open to debate.

Christian shrugged, smiling. "I guess I've already become re-cultured by tech—sushi at funky dive bars and the latest restaurant openings recommended by Eater."

Jillian and Scott raised eyebrows. The trio then settled in with further small talk, clinked their water glasses with a pre-toast, pored over the menu, and bantered with the server before ordering. Jillian and Scott, as was their tradition, would share the wood oven-roasted chicken over bread salad, meant for two. Christian went rogue, again as tradition, with the special of the day, a braised halibut.

After the server collected the menus and left the table, Scott and Christian turned in unison to Jillian, eyebrows raised, not even needing to ask the question.

"It went well," she said, and described the meeting with little embellishment. "Yes, I think it went well. But I'd be surprised if it turned into anything."

Just as she finished her story, the server reappeared, cradling a bottle of Sauvignon Blanc, which he held out to Scott for approval. The gentleman, who likely had been performing this ritual at Zuni for 30 years, took his time, slowly, very slowly, twisting the cork from the bottle neck. He then poured a splash into Scott's glass and waited for the silent nod of approval before filling the others. Jillian shifted in her chair like an antsy child waiting for dessert to be served, anxious for the relief from the wine's warm flush.

Scott raised his glass first. "To my beautiful wife. A woman with conviction and smarts. To you, reinvented. In a startup. One that makes the world a better place."

"Hear, hear," added Christian.

"Well, from your lips to...." She smiled at the two of them as she raised her glass, not finishing the expression. Really, what could go wrong?

CHAPTER 2

S ince the coffee meeting, Jillian had skied the hills of her own confidence. When up, she imagined herself at the top of the startup world, with all its sexiness and crazy risks and rewards. On those days, she reconnected with old contacts on LinkedIn and even did some previously neglected household chores. When down, she saw herself as out-of-place and out-of-date, not skilled enough for the startup world. On those days, she lazily scanned Craigslist and the Whole Foods website for grocery bagger jobs. Half the time she desperately wanted the job at Sojourner. The other half of the time, she would have been relieved to be passed over.

Five days after Desmond Hensley said he'd call, the caller ID she'd been waiting for finally lit up her phone. She was at the gym, but didn't want to let the call go to voicemail. Punching the big red "Stop" button on the treadmill, she jumped off and ducked out the gym's front door to get some privacy, practically whispering, "Hi, Desmond. How are you doing today?"

Desmond got right to business. "Hi, Jillian. I wanted to suggest you come to the office this week and meet the team. We'd need to talk further of course, but I'm thinking you would make a really interesting partner as we ramp up our sales to hotels."

She smiled and leaned back against the gym's exterior wall. "Of course."

"We're not advertising for the role, but I think it would really be smart for us," he continued. "When we meet I'll be able to share with you what I'm thinking and see if it's something that would suit you."

Thank God. They agreed on a time, and she shoved the phone into her pocket and went back inside. This time, she dialed up the speed on the treadmill and burst into a full-on sprint.

When she arrived, Jillian took a moment on the sidewalk in front of Sojourner's building to take stock. She had a picture of a startup's office in her head, and this was not it. The building had an unimpressive lobby, circa 1945, and the elderly doorman did not look up from his crossword puzzle as she entered. When the brass elevator doors opened to the 10th floor, things didn't look any better. At the end of the hall, taped to a door, was the Sojourner logo printed on an ordinary sheet of paper. What was she expecting: ping pong tables and a farm-to-table cafeteria? She didn't need the trappings.

Inside the single room, the clicking of keyboards was the only sound. Desmond had his head in his laptop but looked up and smiled when she entered. Three other men, all dressed like college students in jeans, T-shirts and sneakers, sat in the desks that lined the room. No doubt in warmer weather they would graduate to flip flops. They were probably older than they looked, she thought.

The work stopped and Desmond jumped up.

"Hey, guys. I want you to meet someone. This is Jillian. She has an incredible career in the hotel world, so we've been talking about working together. I wanted her to see the mothership. Such as it is."

He turned to Jillian, smiling, and added, "Actually, we're moving to a WeWork space on the first of next month. We've pretty much outgrown this. There is another developer working remotely right now. But he's in the Bay Area and it would be nice to have more desks so he has the option to come in. Plus conference space. Plus we will be growing the team." He nodded to Jillian as if to indicate her as case-in-point.

"And WeWork has beer on tap," a guy in the corner added. There was chuckling.

"I prefer wine," she said without thinking. She intended the comment to be funny, not literal, but the joke missed the mark and she scolded herself. It pegged her as the classic suburban mom.

Desmond ignored this and introduced her to each employee. The group chatted lightly, and one of the developers asked Desmond about something he was working on. Jillian listened in, not understanding the discussion but pleased with the good nature of their interaction. Finally, Desmond turned and asked, "Can I buy you a cup of coffee?" She said goodbye to the team and they walked out towards the elevator. How did he ever have a private conversation in the office, she wondered.

Desmond leaned forward to press the button and summon the elevator. "Listen, Jillian," he said, "you're the secret weapon we need for signing hotels. I thought we could go to Brew to talk a little more about that."

As they walked, she made a concerted effort to give off a neutral vibe. She was self-conscious about appearing overly eager, needy somehow.

Desmond went into more detail once they settled at a table. "How do you feel about the Head of Partnerships title I mentioned? I think you could be terrific at that. Of course, we'd need to discuss compensation." He stopped. "Which would include equity."

That perfect first date had just turned into a marriage proposal. She knew it was too quick, but she was flattered by the attention. And, honestly, the gold-rush factor of working for a startup was beginning to feel pretty exciting.

"Interested enough to take a look at the job description. But no guarantees." Said aloud, this sounded more hard-to-get than she felt, but that was okay. "Let's talk a little more about your vision for revenue from hotels. We spoke in broad brushstrokes, but I have some ideas I can run past you."

Desmond gave a knowing nod, and they embarked on a substantive discussion about margins, revenue-sharing, hospitality trends, and hotel management structures.

An hour later they were shaking hands as they parted ways. Watching him disappear down the crowded sidewalk, the spring in his step and the messenger bag slung across his back reminded her of Christian when he was younger.

She realized she was grinning widely, then tried to straighten out her face, turned and headed down the sidewalk to BART. Not even the long wait in the station and standing-room-only cars dampened her mood. Once in Berkeley, she made a small detour on her walk home, took a breath before opening the door to On the Board, and stepped in. She was anxious to tell Scott about the meeting.

He was just finishing up with a customer, who passed her with a nod as he exited. Scott's face was a big question mark. "Well?" he asked as they embraced.

She began talking before they even ended their hug. As she described the office and the conversation at Brew, Scott's expression moved from curious, to cautious, to full support.

"What about compensation?" he asked.

This brought her back to earth. "We haven't gotten quite that far. But he said he'd email a job description and I imagine an official offer will come after that."

"Hey, at this point in life, what matters most is not the money. It's that you love what you're doing. Nothing is for-sure solid, nothing is guaranteed," he said. "Not Westbrook. Not some other hotel brand that needs a sales director. Not a bagger position at Whole Foods. So why not jump into something that lights you up? Like Sojourner is seeming to do. And anyway, I'm sure the money will be fine or more than fine."

She hugged him again, harder than she had in a long time.

"So, you know about my bagger-at-Whole-Foods backup plan? Embarrassing. I'll see you at home."

CHAPTER 3

Three days and hours of handwringing later, Desmond sent a draft of the job description, asking for her input. It all seemed right in her wheelhouse. She made a few suggestions, and he answered a couple questions. Then silence—the emails stopped abruptly. He made no move towards a formal job offer, and she purposely wanted him to take the lead while she remained politely encouraging. Maybe he was having second thoughts? She had learned over these last weeks that lack of response usually meant rejection.

So when she saw an email from Desmond in her inbox the next week, she was almost bubbling over. He wanted to meet at the Four Seasons for lunch. Four Seasons? Quite the upgrade from Brew, she thought. He was doing this his way, and that was fine with her.

She arrived first and the maître d' seated her at a window table set for two. The restaurant was on the fifth floor and overlooked Market Street. From this vantage point, she looked below to the crowds of bankers, tech workers and tourists migrating along the sidewalks, a silent river of commerce. She was literally above the fray, an odd disconnect. In the restaurant, everything was restrained, including the decor and the neighboring conversations.

"Don't think the Four Seasons is necessarily Sojourner's style," Desmond said as he approached the table. "But I thought it fitting, considering how important I think our collaboration could be to the company."

She laughed, looking around with approval. "It's one of my favorite places for a quiet conversation or meeting. Though I can't say I got here too often with colleagues, given the fact that it was a competitor to Westbrook."

He sat, and their meeting officially commenced.

Despite Desmond's opening gambit on their possible collaboration, the first 45 minutes of conversation avoided the topic of her employment altogether. Holiday plans. Real estate prices in San Francisco. Whether founders should become politicians. Jillian liked him. She really liked him. He spoke with animation and lightness. There was a safety there, which made her want to come along for the ride. So she nodded to affirm his opinions and contributed her own without fear.

When the remains of her crab salad and his branzino were finally removed from the table, he asked her about dessert. She suggested coffee instead. She knew the plotline: they needed a reason to stay at the table and get on with the purpose of the lunch.

"A green tea for my friend here and a decaf cappuccino for myself," he said to the server.

"Good memory." She wasn't sure if it was demeaning for him to order for her. But he *had* gotten it right, so gave him the credit.

"My memory seems to kick in only when it matters. Anyway, let's talk about Sojourner. I'd love to have you on the team, and you said you're interested, so I took the liberty of preparing a job offer." He reached into his Herschel backpack and passed to her several sheets of paper, flattening them with a quick brush of his palm. She would have used a folder.

"You'll see that the salary we can offer is not what I expect you were earning at Westbrook. But we're all taking haircuts at Sojourner because we believe so much in what we're creating. Including the future value. My dream is that we all become very wealthy. And I see that happening within the next five years. Probably sooner." She looked up and smiled. "Pretty damn cool to do that by helping nonprofits," he added.

The top sheet was titled, "Employment Agreement," and she glanced at the line that specified salary. While she had anticipated a low number, this was less. Which was disappointing. But not a dealbreaker.

"Okay, how about equity?" she asked. Christian had coached her on this conversation. Equity was new territory for her because Westbrook was privately owned, so stock was never an issue with compensation. And, of course, Scott and she had 100 percent ownership of On the Board.

Desmond turned to the second page of the stack, titled "Stock Option Grant Notice." "Here's where that is spelled out. This is a really generous equity offer. You'd be employee number six, in on the ground floor. Future employees will receive significantly less. But as I said, you're really integral to our success with partners, so I wanted to acknowledge that here."

She scanned the numbers and saw 50,000 shares, which was confusing. Guidelines posted online when she'd Googled were percentages: "If you're early to the team, expect equity to be in the range of about 1 percent."

"Um, what percent of the company is the 50,000 shares? And what is the value of each share?"

He paused, then looked her in the eye so directly it made her uncomfortable. "That's not something I can answer because it hasn't yet been determined. Our funding is a convertible note." He stopped talking, gave no explanation, and signaled for the check.

Had it been a stupid question? He had clearly signaled she should not be asking. Anyway, she could take the paperwork home and pore over it with Scott and Christian. Then she would understand the equity terms, no doubt. Including the meaning of *convertible note*.

17

She straightened. "Of course, I'll need some time to think about this and to explore a couple other opportunities I have in progress. How soon are you expecting a response?"

"Well, I would love to know as soon as possible, of course. Say, Friday?"

She didn't really have any other prospects, but she wanted the freedom to weigh this. Plus, she wanted to show him—and maybe herself—that she had options.

"Head of Partnerships, huh?" she asked, turning back to the Employment Agreement. "You've had a while to think on it and the title still fits?"

Desmond nodded. "Yes, I like it. It gives enough information, but also gives us freedom. At some point, we may want to get you involved in selling partnerships or some sort of buy-in to corporate customers, if we go in that direction. It would be a different spin on *partnerships* but it still works. The job description is actually the last pages in the folder, and it's as you've already seen, incorporating your suggestions."

She had spent her career moving from job to job within Westbrook Hotels since she started in her twenties, with no big decisions required. She worked hard. Someone would see potential and tap her for a new role. She'd work hard in that new position. Then a manager a level up would see her potential. Over and over again. Until eventually it was decades later and she had jumped her way to the top. By the end, she had managed a large department with 15 reps and coordinators, an annual budget in seven figures, and a region that included five hotels. This because she had merely accepted what was handed her, in a familiar world. Sojourner felt different. Saying yes to this job required major impetus from within—to jump off a cliff.

"Okay. I will give this consideration and let you know Friday."

This is crazy, she thought as she pushed back from the table. She had an actual job offer in hand. She hadn't dreamed it would be this easy—a couple coffees and a lunch—after no response at all to her other applications. Nor had she dreamed the opportunity would come from a company like this. Yes, she had done the job search grind the last month, networking, sending resumes, scouring LinkedIn. But this was totally unrelated to those efforts, and it felt so easy, so natural, like breast-stroking in a lake with a gentle wind behind.

By the time they reached the ground floor lobby of the Four Seasons and went separate ways, Jillian couldn't wait to be by herself. She craved the freedom to think and process what just happened. First, she'd call Scott.

"Hey, I got the job offer!" she announced as soon as he picked up.

"Honey, that's awesome. I had no doubt."

"Listen, I'm about to go to BART and I want to review the paperwork. Can I fill you in on everything when you get home?" Scott understood about keeping the call short, she thought, as she returned her phone to her bag. He'd know the station would be noisy. Anyway, she wanted to sort things out first in her own mind before giving him the full account.

She walked a block, then down the stairs and an unending escalator to the bowels of San Francisco and the BART platform. A plan began to unfold in her mind. She would cook something special for dinner. Which meant she'd need to stop at Whole Foods on the walk home. But she could have it all prepared by the time Scott got home from work. Having plotted out the next couple of hours, she could relax a little.

Loud announcements of train arrivals and elevators out of service faded to the back of her awareness, as she squeezed into the only empty space on a circular concrete bench. Reaching into her tote for the folder, Jillian peeled it open and began to read the top page line-by-line.

First, the Employment Agreement. Seemed boiler-plate. Benefits standard, including health care. Unlimited vacation. That caused her to take pause. Vacation time at Westbrook Hotels was earned by years of service, but she knew unlimited vacation was in vogue. It sounded great to Jillian, but Christian had warned that it could be deceiving: it actually just protected employers from carrying forward unused vacation days. She'd worked her way up to four weeks vacation at Westbrook. She and Scott had enjoyed taking several trips a year, now that Christian was out of the house. At a startup like Sojourner, that would never fly. Cutting back would be an adjustment. Unless, somehow, unlimited actually meant unlimited? She made a note.

The train approached, and she shoved the paperwork into her bag. It could wait. Pushing her way into the mass of bodies, the train car packed even before rush hour, she hugged her bag to her chest, eager for the quiet comfort of home.

A couple hours later in the kitchen, dinner was well in hand, the aroma of the roasting chicken and root vegetables heavy. Two bakery chocolate cupcakes, each with an inch-deep swirl of frosting, were pushed to the back of the counter, the rare indulgence for dessert. While the lunch with Desmond had energized her, by the time she fought her way through BART, shopped, prepped dinner, and got it into the oven, Jillian was exhausted. She migrated to the bedroom, set an alarm on her phone, and slid under the comforter.

The sound of the front door awakened her. The vestiges of a dream quickly dissipated.

"Scott? Is that you?"

He took the stairs two at a time and bounded into the bedroom. "I asked Jackson to close up. Couldn't wait to hear about your lunch. You were evasive on the phone. So...?"

"Well, I wanted to tell you about it unrushed. And without shouting. Evasiveness unintended."

He threw himself onto the empty side of the bed, shoes still on, propping himself up on one elbow. He'd always been playful that way.

She sat up. "I want to look more carefully through the paperwork before deciding."

"But what does your gut tell you? Do you think you'd love the job? Forget about the details."

Sheepishly, she glanced sideways. "Actually, I think I would."

"Then, I'll pop the Champagne," he said, jumping off the bed with as much energy as he'd jumped onto it. She smiled. He didn't care at all about the salary or details. Well, most likely he did care, but only secondarily. She'd need to ask him about that later but didn't want to spoil the moment. Anyway, she was certainly going to be able to push the company's revenue forward in a big way, which would mean a quick pay raise, or at least a bonus.

She stared at the ceiling, watching a spider make its way to a corner, an inch at a time. Years ago, she would have plotted to kill it, even if beyond her reach. Today, she felt peace in allowing it to have its path.

Glass clinked downstairs as Scott rummaged through the wine refrigerator. "Dinner's in the oven," she called to him, even though it was obvious. Swinging her feet off the bed, she sat for a moment before standing, feeling very grateful. She knew she would take the job.

CHAPTER 4

J illian and Desmond negotiated the final terms of her employment without much drama. Jillian managed to gain a small sum over Desmond's original salary offer. Nevertheless, she was indeed taking a major *haircut,* as she had learned pay cuts were commonly called in the startup world. Balancing that, she still had little understanding of the equity. Christian had walked her through the fine print, and how to calculate the percentage of the company based on the number of shares in the stock option grant. Overall, he was not impressed with the offer. But she believed Desmond when he said it was generous. And anyway, the company was going to scale quickly and the big payoff would be ahead. According to Desmond.

Christian had asked her many questions she did not know the answers to: how much funding had the company secured? Who had invested in the company? How many shares were outstanding? How much monthly recurring revenue did the company have?

She barely even understood the terminology, much less the answers. But she was willing to go forward on trust. Desmond was a good guy. She liked him. She would go with her gut: if she had any indication he was an asshole, she would have walked away. So full speed ahead. She would start in one week.

Once that final week of unemployment was over, Jillian knew she'd need to be all-in. Working at a startup would mean long hours and no days off. So she and Scott took a spontaneous two-day trip to Lake Tahoe. February's snow had been exceptional, and nothing made Scott happier than being out on the slopes. The fact that he owned a snowboard/skateboard shop meant heading to Tahoe was practically a business trip, he always said. And for Jillian, this moment between jobs meant it may be their last opportunity to get away during the week when crowds were thin. Indeed, it may be the last time they could get away at all for a while.

It was two days of focused bliss. Indigo skies. Perfectly groomed trails. A light dusting of fresh snow both mornings. Happy weariness at days' end. Over Old Fashioneds in the dark hotel bar on their last night, they agreed the trip had been just perfect.

After checking out of their hotel (a five-star splurge), they headed back to Berkeley, a little sad. But when the snow was mostly behind them and home still two hours ahead—Jillian and Scott made a last-minute decision to exit I80. They would stop and visit her parents.

In their late 70s, Jillian's parents had just returned from several weeks visiting friends on the East Coast and were still settling back into the routine at their Grass Valley home, where they'd moved for retirement. Jillian understood her parents' motivation to get out of the uber-expensive Bay Area when her father retired from teaching Anthropology at UC Berkeley. But the two-hour drive to Grass Valley meant they saw each other less than when they were just a mile away in Berkeley. And it was enough of a barrier that Jillian sometimes put the trip off.

"Why don't we do this more often?" Scott asked as the car pulled to the stop sign at the end of the exit ramp.

Scott liked her parents and wanted to be involved in their lives and, as they grew older, their care. But his comment fed her guilt about not seeing them enough. Her parents had always been so at-home in the world, something Jillian took pride in. And which let her off the hook somewhat as an only child. They didn't need her, did they? They had their own lives and involvements and passions. Who was she to insert herself into that, which was working so well?

If one were to come upon Janet and Thomas going about their daily lives, say, at the grocery store or at the country club, they looked like they stepped right out of an ad in the AARP magazine—grayed, fit, and well dressed. While their hiking days were over due to knee and hip replacements respectively, they looked like they *could* embark on a hike at any moment (though they'd politely decline with a self-deprecating joke).

Yet in the last year, Jillian had noticed slight changes. They were starting to nap some days. When their beloved black lab passed away, they announced he would be their last pet. Janet commented that their recent trip took a lot out of them.

Jillian didn't want to think of her parents as anything but perfectly capable adults who could take care of themselves, including for two weeks in New England. Scott, however, was more apt to dote on them, to want to baby them.

Jillian's parents were the epitome of a happy couple, but exercised a nice independence from each other. They had separate hobbies—gardening for her and golf for him, somewhat typical for their age—and they were content to spend time together and apart. Jillian knew her mother would welcome more visits, in fact, she teased Jillian about that. Still, Jillian resisted for some reason. She missed the days when her parents were more well-heeled than she and Scott. Back then, Janet and Thomas would invite Scott and Jillian to join them at beautiful new restaurants in the city, and it was assumed they'd be paying, as the parents. Now, her parents seemed to value frugality: "Being on a fixed income, as we are, it makes you pretty careful what you do with your money," they'd say. No more fancy restaurants. More conservative travel. They were down to one car. Her parents' lives now seemed small.

As they pulled into the short gravel driveway, Janet, who was sweeping the little front porch on the stucco ranch house, looked up. She had always been absorbed in her own little world, ever cheerful, even when cleaning, Jillian remembered. Janet waved, all smiles, and Jillian felt even worse that they visited so infrequently.

"Such a wonderful surprise when you called," Janet said as she walked towards the car. Jillian and Scott got out quickly to save her some steps and met her half-way up the front path for the requisite hugs.

"So you had a little getaway?" Janet pulled back to smile at Jillian. "How did the mountain treat you?"

"The knees felt it, that's for sure. At least mine did. Scott's a professional athlete, so he has the knees of a 20-year-old."

"Make that past tense," Scott added, shooting a playful glance at Janet.

"Your father will want to hear all about it. He was just talking about the winter he taught you to ski, Jillian. And when you broke your ankle."

"How *is* Dad?" Jillian asked. "How did the doctor's appointment go?"

Janet stopped short of the porch to answer.

"Not so good." The lightness drained from her face like a filter had been applied. "We're scheduled now for a full dementia assessment next week."

A tangle of thoughts hijacked Jillian's brain. She struggled to unwind them and sort out reality from fear. Finally, she said, "Is it that bad? I mean, forgetfulness is part of aging, for god's sake. I can barely remember where I put my phone these days."

"Honey, yes, it got pretty serious on our trip. When you're out of your familiar surroundings, that's when you really see it." Scott and Jillian caught each other's eyes.

"Oh, Mom. That's so hard." She didn't know what else to add, so didn't.

"Let's not jump ahead. We'll see what happens once we get another opinion."

Her mother was always so level-headed.

Stomping boots on the welcome mat to shake off dirty remnants of snow at the open front door, they could see the back of Thomas's head in the living room. He was reading in his favorite chair in front of the fireplace, still aglow with embers. It would have been a cozy Norman Rockwell scene, a daytime fire on a cold day, had it not been tainted with a conversation about dementia.

Scott didn't hesitate before walking into the living room and circling around the large sofa to meet Thomas face-to-face. "Thomas! Ahoy, mate!" Jillian shot a thankful glance at Janet. She knew Janet adored Scott, and Jillian hoped that Scott's virtue would make up for her hesitance. It was painful to imagine her father as anything but her protector. Thank goodness her mother was there to maintain balance in their lives, to smooth over all the rough ridges. Janet motioned for Jillian to go see her father, and she obediently stepped into the room.

"Hi, Dad. Don't get up." She kissed the top of the head, his hair still thick and wavy at 78, and scooted in next to Scott on the big upholstered ottoman.

Everything seemed normal. He and Scott were comparing notes on the year's snowfall. She studied Thomas's face as he spoke. Was there something missing?

Janet joined them with a plate of cookies and a pitcher of water— always the consummate hostess, even when it was just family. They had a pleasant visit, hearing about the East Coast trip, and Jillian describing their ski getaway. Janet did most of the talking. But then Thomas had never been the talkative one of the pair, so this was not out of the ordinary. Except with the new information about the forgetting.

"How's work, honey?" her father asked. Jillian turned to Scott for a split-second of reassurance. She had not told her parents that she'd resigned from Westbrook. They would worry.

"Oh, same old, same old," she said with a forced smile.

"Well, at least you have a job," her father said. "You've been a star at that hotel for as long as I can remember. I hope they appreciate your loyalty."

She wanted to cringe but maintained the smile. "Right, Dad. I hope they do."

Scott suggested they'd best get on the road to get ahead of the traffic in Sacramento. Jillian loved him so much in that moment. She couldn't wait to leave, yet she couldn't let herself be the one to make the decision.

"Dad, don't get up. See you soon, okay?" she said as she stooped to kiss him again.

She followed her mother out of the room, and Jillian knew that this was how it would be going forward. Her mother shepherding everything. The doctor visits. The social events. The need for naps. The conversations.

Jillian hugged Janet and held that hug longer than she would normally. They had entered some new zone, and it hadn't even been officially named. But Jillian sensed it, knew it was true, that her relationship with her parents was about to change.

"Mom, let me know how the doctor's appointment goes. Or I'll call you. I'm sure they'll find nothing. Just a little forgetfulness." It felt better, somehow, to say this.

"Of course, honey. Hey, I have some biscuits I made this morning. Take them home with you. We can't eat them all. I'll be right back with a few." She disappeared into the kitchen, and Jillian and Scott shared the look that said, "Really? We do not need biscuits." Still, it was the kind thing to do, to accept. So they waited on the porch until Janet emerged with a paper lunch bag, grease stains already starting to show on the brown folds of the bottom.

After the goodbyes, they waved one last time, backing up along the gravel driveway, which was dotted with a few dismal mounds of snow, dirty and crystallized. Jillian reached for a biscuit before they were even to the street, and took a bite. Scott looked at her quizzically but didn't say anything.

"Oh my god, what am I going to do if Dad has Alzheimer's?" she said, finally.

"Even more important, what is your mom going to do? That's a hard road. Though I don't know many women as strong and motivated as your mom at this age. I'm sure she'll handle it with grace."

Jillian didn't want to go there. She took another bite of biscuit. Turning her gaze out the window, she counted her breaths as the snowy landscape turned to green, and hills flattened out to monotony.

CHAPTER 5

O h god, this is like the first day of school, Jillian thought, zipping up her boots.

"You look beautiful." Scott was buttoning a plaid flannel shirt as he watched her dress. He never had to worry about what he wore: when you're the boss and your customers are kids who sport T-shirts adorned in skulls, you get to wear whatever you want.

"And you look smart," he added.

She laughed. Scott learned long ago that she bristled at compliments about beauty, scar tissue from growing up in an era when girls were just starting to get equal treatment. She could still remember when girls weren't even allowed to wear pants to school. Granted, she could *hardly* remember that, but still. It was a thing.

Now she assessed herself in the full-length mirror. Jeans on the first day of work! Her mother would be appalled. At least they were dress jeans. And they were paired with tony boots.

Desmond had told her she could work from home, but for the first few weeks, she wanted to be in the office. After that, they'd be moving to WeWork, and she'd mostly work from home. It would be easier since she would spend much of her days on the phone—which looked to be problematic in a shared space. She had volunteered to use her own laptop and phone, treating the company's budget like her own. She threw both into her tote bag.

Desmond had arranged for Jillian to meet him at 11 o'clock at Brew on her first day of work, a cush start. It was a simple ritual: each signed the employment documentation, page by page, careful to avoid the small spill of coffee on the table. Once complete, Desmond shoved the stack into his backpack with the same disrespect for paper he'd shown before. Then he raised both hands like some kind of blessing: "Well, it's official: welcome to Sojourner!"

Jillian was excited about doing entirely new work. Too many years, she thought, had she catered to the demands of meeting planners—who were always pressing for lower rates and comped amenities, last-minute changes. Today, she was turning that upside down and doing something for people actually in need. Of course, it didn't hurt that Sojourner could eventually bring with it a windfall. She had gained a giddy sense of possibility, not unlike the times she'd bought a Powerball® lottery ticket when the jackpot had run up sky-high.

A few minutes later, they were on the 10th floor, walking down the hallway to the office. He pushed open the door for her, the Sojourner logo hanging askew. Everyone looked up and smiled.

"By the way, do you have an onboarding process?" she asked as she entered.

He stopped. "What do you mean?"

"I just thought there may be a series of meetings. Or ways for me to get up-to-speed quickly."

Clearly this hadn't occurred to him. She glanced around the room. Everyone else was a developer or working on the tech side of things—which they called *product*.

She rescued him from his awkward silence. "Oh, never mind. I'm a total self-starter and will get myself set up. I'll have a plan of attack for partnerships ready for you in a couple days."

"Well, I did have Alex get you on the accounts - G Suite, Slack, Jira, Mailchimp." He seemed proud of that and it allowed him to save face a bit. "Alex will show you how to log in."

"What, no Outlook?" she asked.

Desmond laughed, and then she did too, pretending she'd been sarcastic.

"We have a company T-shirt on order for you," he said. "The first one in a woman's size." Everyone chuckled at that, except Jillian. She cocked her head, perplexed.

"Employee 6. We give each employee a T-shirt with the Sojourner logo and their employee number when they started," Desmond explained. "We all have them."

"Someday—when we're a household name—they'll be priceless," Trevor added.

"Oh," was all Jillian could say.

Desmond motioned to Alex with his head, a silent signal that it was time to get Jillian set up. Alex had one arm tattooed to the wrist, scruffy beard, black T-shirt, and AirPods: in another context, she would have seen him as menacing. It was incredible this new life she was embarking on, this crop of colleagues. He rolled his chair over to Jillian without standing, comical to the outsider but apparently the way they convened in this small room. He held out his hand.

"Welcome aboard. Desmond asked me to get you started," he said, shaking her hand.

Desmond smiled with approval. "Alex will take good care of you, Jillian. Meanwhile, I've got a meeting offsite for the rest of the day. Slack me if you need anything."

She had never even used Slack before. Before she could answer, Desmond had grabbed his backpack and headed back out the door.

"Well, it looks like you're my man, Alex," she said. "Can you walk me through what I need to know?" He gestured to a chair to indicate it was hers and waited as she reached for her laptop.

Thirty minutes later, Alex had her all set up so she could access a collection of apps on her laptop. He scooted himself back to his corner, and she stared into her screen, paralyzed as to what she should do next. She opened a Google doc. Thank goodness it looked like a pared-down Microsoft Word document. She typed out, "Quarterly Objectives," then sat back to think about how she wanted this to work.

Meanwhile, Slack notifications began popping up. She hesitated a moment before she clicked on one and read a thread between Trevor and Alex. Then some chatter about a feature Trevor and Nate were working on. This amused her, since the developers all sat within a few yards of each other, minus the remote guy. Yet, the only sound in the room was keyboards clicking and occasionally a chair rolling back.

She sighed. Then she typed out a message to the channel labeled "#general," requesting an hour from each to learn more about their work. This would be her DIY onboarding process.

"Please feel free to put a time on my calendar that's convenient for you. And we can meet at Brew, if you're in the office. Otherwise, I'll try my hand at a Slack video call." Did they use emojis here? She played it safe and went without.

For the remainder of the day, she plodded away at her planning document. Her eyes frequently skirted the edge of her screen, checking the time. Without meetings and clients' fires to put out, which she was accustomed to at Westbrook, the clock seemed stuck. This wasn't what she'd been expecting at a startup. It was a little quieter, much more subdued. All heads-down work. Where was the living-on-the-edge energy? Of course, that would probably change, once she got more involved. When Desmond was in the office, and of course when they moved to WeWork, things would get livelier. After all, WeWork was the epitome of startup life. As Trevor had pointed out: Free Beer! That was the cornerstone of good work, right? Jillian shrugged at the ridiculousness of that thought.

She took another glance at the time to be absolutely sure it was after 5, stood, and packed up her things. The rest of them never looked up as she left the office.

Christian phoned just as Jillian and Scott finished dinner.

"So…?"

"Let's just say it was a slow start," she said. As Jillian described her day to Christian, she sank into the chair. Starting this work was like taking a locomotive from 0 to 60 mph. A ton of coal would be required, and she would be shoveling it alone. But she wanted to put a positive spin on it for Christian. "I'm totally up to the challenge. It's just a very different environment. I need to be self-driving," she said after explaining.

"You always complained about your coworkers at Westbrook. At least at Sojourner you're in full control of your destiny."

"I get it. I'm just saying I'm going to need to focus on staying motivated and productive. It has to come from within, at a company like this."

"Maybe you need more time with Desmond. I thought he was quite high-spirited when I met him."

"One hundred percent," she said. "I scheduled an hour with him tomorrow."

"Good. Side note: maybe now that you're an employee, you can ask for more details about funding status. We call it runway. You know, like for planes? It's the time you have ahead before you'll crash and burn. When he was pitching to us, he said he was closing a round in Q2. Q2 is around the corner."

"Do I really want to know? After all, I'm on the plane. The plane is accelerating down the runway. It's in the pilot's hands, not mine." She regretted the continuation of the runway metaphor.

Christian hesitated. "Huh? Anyway…if runway is an issue, you can help him. Or, worst-case scenario, you can assume the crash position. Oh my god…." He laughed. "This is way out of control."

"Well, yeah, it's a troubling visual. But you make a fair point." She did not want to know, and Desmond had skillfully deflected her previous questions, including the one during her interview, a detour she was happy to succumb to at the time. Yet, she knew Christian was right. "I'll see if I can find an opening. Or maybe I'll ask someone else. I'm doing one-on-ones with everyone this week."

"The most common reason startups fail is that they run out of money," he said.

That would not happen to Sojourner. She was sure of it, with only the smallest sliver of doubt.

When they hung up, Jillian poured herself another glass of wine and ruminated on the sofa while Scott finished the dishes. She had the power to make a positive impact on Sojourner's viability. After all, that's why sales was such a key role. She'd just need to perform. Create some miracles. Which hopefully she could do. Well, of course she could do it. Hopefully.

"You're going to do better than you think," Scott said over his shoulder, the water still running.

"I've got to say, it's unnerving to know you have a limited bank account to work with, but you don't know the balance. You've gone out of your way to support me, too, but you admitted things are getting tight at On the Board with the rent increase. And you don't have much fat to cut. Which means the only way we can make up the difference is to hit a home run at Sojourner." She stared into her wine glass.

Scott was nodding as he wiped his hands on the nubby dishtowel. "Okay, maybe so. But let me worry about that. You just do what you're best at."

She'd need to turn off the voices in her head if she wanted to create miracles. There could be no room for doubt. *That* she was sure of.

CHAPTER 6

By Friday of Week Two, Jillian felt she'd made a massive amount of progress. A hefty document laid out her strategic plan. She'd reached out to 30 hotel contacts to set up meetings. She'd met with each person at Sojourner to learn about his role and perspectives on the company. She'd volunteered to head up the office move and took over the negotiations with WeWork to finalize Sojourner's contract, as well as moving logistics. She liked being in a flat organization where she could pitch in for anything, even admin-level tasks. From what she could tell, there was no org chart and everyone reported to Desmond, like she did.

Her biggest win, though, came unexpectedly: Desmond invited her to join him at an investor pitch meeting.

"Having you there will lend gravitas to our message," he said. "Joe Chan is a luminary among VCs, and I can't believe we got an appointment at Ciera Capital."

Did *gravitas* refer to credibility—or was it age? She was unsure, and it unsettled her a bit. In the end, she decided to disregard the comment.

The day before the meeting, she Slacked Desmond to ask when they'd prepare. "We'll wing it," he replied. "You're a total natural at meetings like this. Don't worry. Just follow my lead." Winging it was not her idea of how to go into a meeting like this. She liked to prepare thoroughly for important meetings, and she couldn't think of anything more important than fundraising. Plus, her nerves were on edge—she had no idea what a meeting like this would be like, not to mention what would be expected from her. But he was the boss, and he had done this before. He apparently didn't think prepping together was necessary or that the meeting was a big deal—despite his amazement that they got the appointment—so she let it go.

But she figured out a Plan B and made a call—to Christian. She asked him what VCs cared about, how Christian thought she could best contribute to an investor meeting. She also wanted his feedback on Desmond's pitch style.

"Well, I'd have to say Desmond was very friendly when he pitched us, easy to have a conversation with. The guy was smooth, in a very casual, we're-just-bros-chatting-it-up kind of way. And we left the meeting having a very positive feel for the company. Interested, I'd even say. But in the follow-up, before we even got to due diligence, there were some holes, so we moved on."

"You're being elusive, Christian. What kind of holes?"

"If there had been a serious problem, I would've urged you not to join the company. Just didn't have a solid feeling about some of his responses to questions—and a couple other companies had caught our attention by that point—so we passed."

So while it sounded a little loose to her, Desmond's style was acceptable, or at least so thought Christian. She would not worry. She continued.

"Okay, so what do investors look for in a pitch meeting?"

"That's easy. A concise and clear presentation is important. Usually, the information goes like this: you tell a story about how you or someone else experienced a problem, then you outline the extent of the problem, and then show how the product solves the problem.

Basically, you tell the story and you show the numbers: market size, current revenue, projected revenue."

Pretty straightforward. That made her feel better.

"What do you think I can bring to the table for Sojourner's pitch?"

"Well, I don't know a ton about the business and only the basics of what you've told me about your role, so I really don't know." He thought a minute. "But off the top of my head, I'd think you guys would want to show off what you, Jillian Johnson, are bringing to the company, that you have deep experience and a network in hospitality."

"Okay, yeah. That I can do. I think." She hung up feeling only slightly better.

The next morning, the team was circled up in the tiny office for the weekly team all-hands meeting, backs to their desks like a high-tech campfire. Jillian could see from the corner of her eye that Desmond, laptop on his knees, was moving graphic elements around in a slide deck—most likely for the pitch meeting—while Trevor spoke about development work that had been completed in the prior week. Desmond retyped some numbers, then tweaked them again, oblivious to Trevor's presentation. Trevor seemed not to notice the lack of attention, or if he did notice, he must not have cared. Was her irritation a holdover from common etiquette lessons from the last century? Maybe Desmond was better at multitasking and was actually listening. She dismissed it and tried to focus on Trevor's words.

The investor meeting was scheduled for 4 p.m. that afternoon, at an office about five blocks from theirs in the Financial District. By 3:30 she was itching to go and Slacked Desmond. "Ready to head out?"

"I'm in the middle of something. We don't need to leave until 3:45."

At 3:47 she pushed back her chair, put on her coat, and stood next to his desk, where she could see he was still working on the deck.

"I know, I know," he said as he shut his laptop cover and threw it into his backpack. "We'll take an Uber."

Jillian liked to arrive early to meetings. She guessed Desmond might call that a waste of time. Perhaps true, but she liked to start high-pressure situations with calm confidence, not in a rush. Just one more mindset change she'd need to make. At Sojourner—or was it at startups as a whole?—there was much more of an on-the-fly, fast pace. They walked in the doors of Ciera Capital at 4:01.

In the Uber on the way to the meeting, Desmond had finally prepped Jillian about how the meeting would go, his pitch, and how she should participate. The hasty conversation yielded a very rough plan as they drove the five blocks: when Desmond presented the business model, he would ask her to add her comments and insights. She suggested adding her experience at some point, and he agreed.

Good. It was doable, even if a little late. She prepared several talking points in her head, wanting to make a solid impression. Plus, she'd need an opportunity to demonstrate her hospitality expertise, as Christian had advised.

After checking in at the white marble reception desk, a polished receptionist ushered them down a long hall. Each conference room they passed had a name inscribed on a brushed metal plate, all elite university nicknames. Cardinal. Quakers. Crimson. Fighting Irish. They were led into Big Blue, and the receptionist said Mr. Chan would be with them momentarily, before turning to leave Jillian and Desmond alone. Wanting to follow Desmond's lead, Jillian watched as he selected one of the Aeron chairs, and she sat next to him. Desmond leaned forward onto the glass table and scrolled through his phone, his body language relaxed. In a way that relaxed Jillian, too. Obviously, she was making too much of this meeting in her head. She looked around. The room had all the technology and none of the warmth she was accustomed to in a hotel meeting room. The quiet heaviness felt a little like waiting for the judge in a courtroom.

Minutes later, Joe Chan entered. A partner at the firm, he looked to be about 30, in pressed jeans and a checked shirt, the business casual uniform of the era. Most likely he had graduated at the top of his MBA class at Stanford or an Ivy League school, the CV of the Valley. Yet he seemed affable enough.

The three chatted about the rain and the drive to the office, then Desmond transitioned artfully, connecting his phone via Wi-Fi to the oversized screen on the wall to begin his pitch. She marveled that he did this without a hiccup; she had trouble changing input modes on their TV.

Desmond began with his origin story, how he hatched the concept behind Sojourner after spending a series of bored evenings in his hotel room in New York. For a moment Jillian wondered if this was actually true—from what she knew of how he got the idea, it was more theoretical, less of an experience. But she figured it didn't matter. This was a better story. She had known some good salespeople who stretched the truth for impact. And while it wasn't her style, she could overlook it.

Desmond then outlined how the company was structured and concepts behind the business model. Pretty much what Christian had told her was standard. She straightened when the business model slide came up, waiting for her cue. But the cue didn't come. He explained, then moved to the meat of the pitch: the projected size of the market and revenue forecast for Sojourner. Perhaps there was a slide a little later that would circle back to the business model, and that was where she was supposed to contribute?

Meanwhile, Jillian was surprised when she saw the market size number on the screen as Desmond described how he did the math. Because this was not an existing market, the calculations involved triangulating several pieces of data. And one of these was one she knew well: the business traveler universe. He overstated this and had been overly generous in his calculation of the number of travelers that would participate in a program like Sojourner's. He also embellished the hotel industry's marketing spend.

She refocused, readying herself for Desmond's signal to comment.

But he continued. She waited. For a moment, she considered interrupting, but that wouldn't be right. It was her first investor meeting. He knew what he was doing; perhaps there was a reason he didn't tag her. Maybe her cue was ahead?

Several slides later, Desmond closed his laptop and grinned. "We think Sojourner is the most exciting new idea for business travel since the expense account, and we'd love to have your investment."

Jillian looked down at her hands. The ball would not be thrown to her.

Joe Chan smiled politely. "I do have some questions.... For instance, what's your moat? Especially since this is not strictly a software play, what prevents another company from duplicating the concept and building it faster than you can?"

"Right. I'll let Jillian field that."

She looked up, startled. What was he thinking? She had never even heard the term *moat* until the day before, when Trevor had briefed her on this idea that startups need to have a product or market that is defensible—some factor that precludes competitors from overtaking them, like a moat protecting a castle from invasion.

"That's an excellent question, but not one that worries us," she began, recomposing herself. "I have been deep in this world for decades, and I've already built a structure at Sojourner that will allow us to partner with 500 U.S. hotels and market to their business traveler guests. Which will allow us to fill the events easily. Which will expand the appeal to an even broader range of hotels."

Joe nodded as if he agreed, even though she knew he could poke holes all over this explanation if he tried. The fact that he was moving on to a question about software told her he was only mildly interested.

Finally, when their scheduled 30 minutes were up, Chan stood and thanked them. "It's an interesting idea. We have a partner meeting every Tuesday and I'll present it to them, then get back to you with feedback."

When they reached the sidewalk in front of the building,

Desmond suggested they walk back to the office. He bubbled. "I thought that went really well. An investment from Ciera would be huge. I think it's highly possible we'll get it."

Jillian had a very different reading on Chan's response but was unsure whether to say that. Did she have enough experience to even offer an opinion on this? Finally, she decided to keep quiet. Chan would do what he was going to do, whether or not she said anything. She hoped she was wrong.

Instead, she took a risk about something else. "Your numbers are a bit high on the business traveler market. The figures I've seen on that are about 30 percent lower. You might want to tweak that for the next pitch."

"Oh, founders inflate numbers all the time. Believe me, if you don't, you're going to be outpitched by someone who does."

She didn't want to be a Pollyanna, but honesty mattered to her. They were in the do-the-right-thing business, after all. She picked up the pace of their walk. "You run the risk of having it catch up with you, though," she added.

"How so?"

"I don't know; if the VC is interested and digs deeper, wouldn't it come to light in due diligence?"

Desmond shrugged it off and changed the subject.

The noise of the city grated on Jillian as they walked, and the sudden siren of a passing fire truck rattled her. She craved the quiet, leafy block of her home in Berkeley, far enough from downtown that the occasional barking dog was the extent of the audio assault.

"Hey listen," she said. "I'm going to take off from here and work the rest of the day at home. I'm in the office tomorrow, so let's spend an hour processing the meeting. I'd like to know how I can contribute better on these investor calls."

As expected, the suggestion received a lukewarm reception. Jillian turned and walked away, voices in her head talking nonstop to divert attention from the unsettled sensation in her gut.

CHAPTER 7

J illian had read enough personal growth books to know she was a kinetic learner: she really "got" things best with activity, by doing. So she knew an immediate priority should be to participate in an actual nonprofit's event booked through Sojourner. She wanted to see for herself what was working well, and to collect some anecdotal talking points to use on sales calls. It was one of her secret sales weapons: to talk about real situations, rather than theoretical, as she pitched. Much more colorful. Stories got the sale.

Jillian logged into Sojourner and looked at the Events section on the dashboard. One stood out: Moms United for Veterans. The event had a lot of things going for it: the date was coming up and the nonprofit was already on her radar (who *doesn't* want to support veterans?). Icing on the cake: it would be held in The Broderick, a posh property South of Market that was a favorite of the tech community and where she already had a great relationship with the sales director.

She made a phone call and it was all set up. Jillian would arrive a half hour early so she and Marlene Michaels could catch up. That would leave plenty of time for Marlene to assist in the room setup and put any finishing touches on the arrangements with the client.

On the evening of the event, Jillian stayed late in the office—or at least it was late for her. She wanted to be at The Broderick by 6:30, and as she closed her laptop and stuffed it into her tote, the developers were still at their desks and engrossed in their screens with no signs of packing up. Kind of impressive. Maybe she should release the irritation she felt almost daily when they sauntered in at 10 or 11. They were putting the time in, just on a different clock, right?

Desmond, however, was nowhere to be seen. She'd hoped to touch base with him before heading over to the event, to get any background on the veterans association, which he'd lined up as a partner. *Where was he, anyway?* She headed out the door.

A five-minute walk later, Jillian moved through the revolving door into The Broderick's lobby and was surprised to be greeted by an awaiting Marlene.

"Jillian! Welcome. You look spectacular." Marlene offered a quick semi-hug, turned, and motioned for Jillian to follow.

"You guys just can't stop the buzz about this place, can you?" Jillian commented as they walked to the escalators. "Looks like all the hipsters are here for cocktails."

Marlene's second-floor office was so understated that it was classy—white leather furniture, a few over-sized black-and-white framed photos, and touches of brass here and there. The rest of the sales staff had obviously gone home, and the warren of offices was still. Marlene gestured for Jillian to sit. "How long have you been at Sojourner? I have to admit, I was happy to see you'd joined up. It sounds like a really exciting job. Honestly, I wish I'd seen it advertised."

Jillian smiled like an apology. "Oh. Well, it wasn't advertised. I was introduced to the CEO, and 'the rest is history,' as they say."

She supposed that was true. She just didn't want to say her son introduced them. She liked to think she got the job through networking, which of course she totally did. Once Christian gave her Desmond's contact information, it was all on her. No favors. No nepotism.

"What's it like at a startup?" Marlene asked. "Do you have a chef, laundry service, and all those perks I keep reading about?"

Jillian laughed. "No, none of that. It's a regular job, just a very small team."

"Well, I'm sure you have the prospect of getting a big windfall at some point. Imagine Sojourner getting acquired. Or even an IPO...."

Jillian looked at Marlene with raised eyebrows. "Marlene, do you really think a company that helps nonprofits is going to IPO? I want Sojourner to be fiscally healthy, but I don't see this as a unicorn."

This was something Jillian had been thinking about. Desmond always talked about what he called "a jackpot" ahead. Yet much of their mission was to help nonprofits. There was a disconnect there: jackpot versus nonprofits. But Jillian had managed to shelve this thought quickly whenever it came up. With Marlene, she went with the higher ground story.

Marlene sighed. "I guess you're right. Grass is always greener, right? Anyway, congrats. So far everything with Sojourner has gone well for us. There are some things I wish the platform did better, but they're not a huge deal...."

Jillian interrupted. "Oh, I'm sorry. Like what?"

"Well, it's fine. Even Facebook and Google have their issues. The bottom line is that we've had very good participation from our guests, and they review the experience really well. And that's what really counts. For us, it's all about offering extra value to our best customers. Let's go check out the room, and I'll introduce you to the executive director of the nonprofit."

It was a tiny meeting room, tucked in the far corner of the floor, one unlikely to be utilized at night, Jillian thought. Exactly the point that made Sojourner a good opportunity for hotels. The feeling was pleasant when they walked in. The room had been set up mostly with high tops, very casual. At the back was a small bar that was clearly going to be self-service—no bartender prepping, and several bottles of red and white wines were lined up open and corked, as well as an array of bottled waters and a pretty arrangement of glasses with cocktail napkins. Along the far side of the room, two tables were pushed together to form what looked to be an assembly line, with five or six open cardboard boxes on the spread, and a few beneath the tables. Marlene explained that the guests would first hear from the executive director about the mission of the organization and what they do, and then they would be assembling backpacks with school supplies for kids.

Behind them, a woman rushed in, out of breath. "So sorry I'm later than I planned to be. I swear the bus moved half a block in 30 minutes." She held out her hand, "I'm Natalie. MUV's executive director."

Marlene welcomed her and introduced Jillian, explaining why she was there. Natalie seemed appreciative but preoccupied, which Marlene picked up on. "How can we help you set up?" she asked.

As they got to work arranging the boxes, Natalie explained that they used these backpacks for military families relocating mid-year. The kids appreciated receiving a gift, which softened the transition. And parents appreciated not having to shop. "We usually make these during the summer, for back-to-school," she said, "but we just received a major in-kind donation from an office supply company, so it was worth it to assemble them now."

Before long, hotel guests began trickling in. Marlene excused herself and Jillian stationed herself near the bar, smiling but not striking up any conversations, wanting to be an observer. The guests were mostly middle-aged men, probably business travelers with hotel loyalty program status. There was also a couple in their twenties, and a mom with a teenage son. Interesting. Not all business travelers. Then Jillian remembered Marlene had mentioned the marketing department had promoted the event in the 12th-floor lounge, where breakfast and happy hour service were included for a premium room. That explained the skewed demographic, for sure. Most of the attendees had helped themselves to a glass of wine or water and were chatting amongst themselves.

After clearing her throat to get their attention, Natalie gave a nice little speech. She had crafted a compelling message—anyone would resonate with the stories about how grateful the children were to receive these backpacks in the past. Jillian looked around the room, and by the rapt looks on the faces, everyone there was probably a parent— with the exception of the twenty-somethings.

After a little instruction on the assembly project, the group got to work and chatted noisily as they assembled the backpacks. Jillian helped take the completed backpacks and load them into larger plastic bins Natalie had brought. Even Jillian was feeling lifted by the energy in the room. She smiled at Natalie, "Great presentation, and such great work you're doing." She'd wanted to say something more profound, but that was what came out.

The assembling went quickly, and before an hour was up, the backpacks were complete. The attendees stopped to speak with Natalie on their way out, several taking her business card. Meanwhile, Jillian cleaned up the extra Moms United for Veterans fliers that had been left behind, then helped organize the boxes of pencils and a few stray crayon boxes.

Once everything was packed, Jillian couldn't help but ask Natalie about her Sojourner experience. "I mean, is there anything that didn't work as you expected, or any improvements we could make?"

Natalie looked for a second at the floor before answering, still not meeting Jillian's eyes. "Listen, we had a great turnout. I think the guests were pretty into it, and some of them may even become donors. So that's all a win. But to be perfectly candid, we did have some problems with the system." She paused, finally looking at Jillian, as if for reassurance.

"No really, it's fine. That's why I'm here. We need to know."

The system had frozen several times as they'd tried to book the room. She had used the chatbot to ask for help, but no one had ever responded. "Luckily, I tried again the next day, and the platform was back up. Working fine."

Jillian scrambled for the words to explain. "I'm so sorry. That shouldn't have happened. Obviously. I know we're weak on the helpdesk side of things. Which is no excuse. I'll bring this feedback back to the team, and that'll light a fire on the service. And preventing site crashes, like the one you experienced."

Natalie smiled pleasantly. "No worries. We got it done. And now I've got a nice evening ahead of me. So great to have a short event that gets a lot done and increases our donor base. Thank you!"

Jillian had learned a lot. She would, she told herself, put the bugs Natalie described out of her mind until the morning. Because she too had a whole night ahead. She texted Scott. "Hey. I know it's crazy, but do you want to see a movie? I could meet you at 8 at the Rialto." For some reason, she didn't want to think too much for the rest of the evening.

CHAPTER 8

*C*ompany *offsite and teambuilding activity! Save the date! Details to come!*

Desmond had sent the Slack message with much fanfare—and assorted emojis. However, as the scheduled date approached, details of the event were *not* forthcoming. Jillian held back. It was an irritation she didn't care to take on, and no doubt it would all come together. "Not my problem," she said to herself at one point.

The night before the date, she opened a message sent from Desmond to @everyone that started: "Our Epic Offsite." In it, he instructed everyone to meet at the Victory Hotel at 10 a.m. After a session there, they would walk to a VR studio and play a virtual reality game, then return for lunch and the rest of the afternoon.

"Crap," she said out loud. VR—not her world. All the others had grown up immersed in video games—still were. Her experience didn't go much beyond Centipede and Frogger. She would be totally out of her element. Would her performance be judged? Would they think less of her? Her brain felt tight just thinking about it, though the irony amused her: the purpose of the day was to build collaboration, and here she was worried about her personal performance. At least the rest of the day would be back at the meeting room, where she felt much more comfortable.

By the next morning, Jillian had let go of the performance anxiety. *It is what it is. I'll handle it. It's supposed to be fun.* These words pulsed gently through her brain like mantras as she got off the train and walked to the address Desmond had given. The hotel had only been open a month, so she was curious.

The lobby—wow! Not your grandfather's hotel. The decor bordered on Goth: black walls, heavy black furniture with antiqued silver trim, a few pillows of blood red. A huge iron light fixture, strung up with a series of chains, hung low in the center. It didn't seem that long ago that hotels were designed to feel like cozy living rooms, with tufted sofas, dark paneling, and classics-filled bookcases. This was quite a departure from that. She had to admit, though, that it was cool.

Jillian stopped to survey the room and look for the elevator bank. A too-friendly, "How may we help you?" was lobbed from the front desk by a woman who looked just out of college, her hair drawn tight in a springy ponytail. *Why hadn't they gone full-on Goth vibe with the front desk staff? Missed opportunity. And guests should not be assaulted—only be addressed when they approached.* She'd been in the hotel business too long—critiques were instinctual.

"I'm good," Jillian said with a forced smile, as she caught the glint of the elevators to the left. She had been to enough hotel meetings to find the room she needed without the assistance of a teenager. On the way, she passed the standard brass marquis with an Events of the Day printout. Sojourner: Third floor, Triumph Room.

Once upstairs, she was the first to arrive at the room. She surveyed the conference table, subconsciously weighing the benefits of position and selected a chair just to the side of the table's head, facing the door. Thankfully, coffee service was set and Jillian went over to pour herself some hot water and inspect the tea offerings.

Good quality, but not five-star. She poured her cup and retreated to her place at the table to wait for it to cool a bit.

As Jillian was setting up her laptop and notebook, Trevor poked his head in the door, then pushed it fully open and came in. He looked to each corner of the room.

"Oh, hey. Figures you'd be the only one here."

"What's *that* supposed to mean?" She winked after she said it, unsure whether he'd recognize she was teasing. She was still feeling her way around the humor culture at Sojourner.

"We are not exactly punctual as a company. It's always bugged me. So I'm glad you tend to be on time. A responsible type."

"Yeah, I do like the gold stars. Unfortunately, what was rewarded in school isn't necessarily rewarded in business, I've found." Again, she kept a smile to indicate it was a joke, though only kind of. He put his backpack on a chair and headed to the coffee and pastries.

"Sojourner would work better if we acted a little more like we cared about the gold stars. In my humble opinion," Trevor said. "I try to write very clean code, and deadlines matter a lot. That stuff should carry through to other areas. I just think the company could work at a higher level." As Trevor poured his coffee and doctored it with cream and several packets of sugar, the others began to drift in.

Jillian was taken aback at Trevor's candor, as well as his inclination towards excellence. They were on the same page. Since starting at Sojourner, she hadn't trusted her gut. She was never sure if the gap between what she thought *should* happen and what *did* happen was a true gap, or whether it was more an indicator of working in an all-new culture. A culture with a different code of conduct.

Jillian wished she felt more comfortable with her co-workers and would have thought she'd have made more progress by now. In her hotel job, she liked lunches and one-on-one coffees to connect with colleagues, but the culture at Sojourner didn't allow for that. Everyone ate alone, mostly at their desks while looking at Instagram, and as far as she could tell, no one socialized after work either. Scott suggested she initiate lunches or drinks, but it felt too awkward. She didn't want to buck the status quo just a few weeks into her tenure.

Finally, Desmond entered with a flourish. He went straight to the head of the table and set up his laptop with an intensity like he was the only one in the room. Apparently, he would forgo coffee and breakfast. Then, like he just realized he had an audience, he looked up and smiled at everyone around him. Everyone else straightened to attention on cue.

He welcomed the group in a classic put-on leader tone, then spoke for a few minutes about the goals for the meeting. He had clearly Googled *offsite icebreakers,* because then they went around the room and answered the question, *What work are you most excited about this year?* An hour later, Jillian couldn't even remember any of the answers. By the time they'd all spoken, Desmond closed his laptop. It was time to leave for the VR activity. *That hour was a waste*, Jillian thought. She would offer to plan the next offsite meeting.

The walk to the VR space was two blocks, and the group naturally broke into twos and threes as they wove through the busy sidewalks. Trevor seemed to make a point of being at Jillian's side. His comments on a Doberman they passed alerted Jillian to the fact that he had a soft heart for all dog breeds, as she did. There was satisfaction in finding something in common outside work.

After a few minutes of waiting in the small lobby of "It's Virtual," a man came out from behind the check-in desk. He cleared his throat and opened his arms to get their attention. With Eastern European features, a neatly trimmed beard and the gold plastic name tag that read "Ivan, Manager." he looked more like a bouncer at a fancy club than a middle-of-the-day lackey at a teambuilding venue. Of course, it had been decades since Jillian had even seen a bouncer, a thought that slightly dismayed her.

"Okay, Team Sojourner. In just a moment we'll be ready for you to start the Davy Jones Locker experience."

Jillian chided herself for not having seen the *Pirates of the Caribbean* movies. According to the poster that dominated one wall, "The experience immerses players in a familiar but new take on the world of pirates, as you pillage Caribbean villages and amass riches and gold." She had no idea what that meant.

With a whoosh, the double doors to the room opened wide, and Ivan planted himself at the entrance. "Team Sojourner, please enter. I will be outfitting you with the VR equipment and explaining the rules of the game once you're inside."

Alex and Nate gave each other high-fives like they were going to rule this game. These guys had no doubt played more games concerning pirates in the last year than she had in her lifetime. Which was zero. Of course, she had one thing up on them: she'd been on Disneyland's Pirates of the Caribbean ride before they were even born. Actually, before Johnny Depp was born. Back when it was just a ride, and not yet a ride-turned-into-a-movie. Maybe that counted for something. Of course it didn't, but it amused her.

Ivan rolled a cart filled with headsets, swords, and pistols into the room, and the guys gathered around, abuzz. Jillian recoiled when Nate joked, "Selfie time!" Thank god he seemed to be kidding. She'd be mortified if one of them posted a photo on LinkedIn or the company website. It's one thing to leave traditional hospitality for a startup, and quite another to be spotted on the Internet, gaming alongside a group of 20-somethings. It was the same discomfort she felt once in a Forever 21 store when she ran into her admin, who was…21.

They were to keep their headsets on 100 percent of the time, Ivan said, as he distributed the equipment. No one could leave the room, except in an emergency, and for their safety they were not to step past the large square painted on the floor, their boundaries for the game. They had 50 minutes to locate the treasure.

"Is the treasure in Davy Jones' locker?" Jillian asked.

Ivan looked at her with disdain. "Davy Jones was a mythical figure who transported the dead, and where the souls were kept, not a treasure." She shrunk at her misstep, glad to be invisible behind the headset.

A warning signal would go off, Ivan announced, when 10 minutes remained. And there was a virtual clock on the mast of the pirate ship they would be seeing in the VR. If they didn't locate the locker by the time the clock made its final buzz, they lost the game.

"Ohhhhh," moaned the group. From this collective sarcasm, Jillian could tell the guys took this seriously. And they thought there was no way they would lose.

Once Ivan exited—"Good luck, Team Sojourner," he said as the door closed behind him—Jillian froze, unsure what would come next. She had never done an escape room, much less VR, and had only recently even heard of this form of entertainment from Christian.

Ivan must have flipped a switch because the room around her transformed to a rustic galleon's deck. Her teammates were gleefully checking themselves out, as they were now muscular pirate types with feathered hats and old-timey pistols. She wasn't quite sure who was who. She looked down. Her own virtual get-up was a cross between Blackbeard and a madame of the Wild West, which started her laughing, too.

Suddenly, cannon fire exploded from a nearby man-of-war. She shrunk at the blasts, while the others immediately fired back, managing to quiet the enemy. Still unsure what was real and what wasn't, on edge, she began to explore. As she felt her way along the wharf, Alex yelled from the other side of the room: he found a clue. They all made their way to him tentatively, still not having their VR legs. A cadre of ghosts appeared from nowhere and gunfire burst out again. This time, Jillian got off a few rounds. The phantoms disappeared, hit.

Alex's clue turned out to be a series of numbers on a small sign, hand-painted in virtual blood. At first Alex thought the numbers were dates, but they weren't. Jillian saw a padlock on a treasure chest along the far wall. It occurred to her that the numbers Alex found could very well relate to the combination to open it. But how? Maybe they could fire bullets to manipulate the numbers in the combination. She called that out, and a couple people gave her back slaps as they gathered around.

Then Desmond shouted that they could use every third number—which made sense because there were dashes. Jillian nodded and tried exactly what he called out. Voila! The chest opened, and inside were three coins. Alex pushed his way past. "This can't be the treasure," he yelled. Relieved to be out of the spotlight, Jillian stepped back to watch the others shout out ideas. Then, discouraged, they dispersed in silence across the room to stumble upon other clues.

When the 10-minute warning buzzer reverberated, the anxiety level in the room rose palpably, but Jillian hung back and resisted the frantic search. They were close to finding the treasure, or so it felt, because they had solved several clues. Jillian wasn't sure, though, if she would know it when they found it. Someone said that it looked like there were three more clues. There was frantic rushing, with rounds of shooting as they fended off attacking marauders.

After what seemed like just a couple minutes, the final buzzer blared, letting all the energy out of the room. The guys' shoulders fell in defeat. Failure.

Meaningless, thought Jillian, her heart not in it.

As someone in the control room (presumably Ivan) flipped a switch, the pirate-ship backdrop fell away and Team Sojourner was now just six people suited up in black gear and headsets. Desmond stepped to the center of the group's circle and tried to keep everyone pumped up. "Hey guys, we did great! We almost got out! Hardly anyone does! Well done!" Jillian felt the hollowness of this, and when she looked around at the faces as they pulled off their headsets, she knew they felt it, too. No one was happy to see Ivan, when he came in to show them what they'd missed and offer his consolation, too.

"Drinks for everyone," Desmond shouted afterwards and then realized it was only 11 am. "Well, tonight!" he added, embarrassed.

Now he would have to rally the troops for the rest of the meeting, Jillian thought. Which would be tough. Another event planning misstep. Presumably, next up was lunch. And then? They had four hours to fill. She wasn't sure this group had the attention span to talk about the business for an extended period.

They trudged back to the hotel, gloomy from the defeat, taking their seats around the conference table. Jillian wondered why lunch was not set up. If she was hungry, she imagined the growing boys were, too. Meanwhile, Desmond made a heroic effort to rally the morale, though not entirely successful. She pitched in, offering an upbeat reflection on how well they did with collaboration, and it was this key quality needed for success in the next phase of the company's growth.

The faces around the table were on board with her message, but Jillian felt they were quietly resisting, too. She knew they really wanted to win as individuals. Jillian just wished she could get them to see that if they relinquished this they would actually win as a team. So she felt deflated, too, as they moved on to another topic. In the background, the hotel staff began setting up the lunch buffet, clanking cans as they arranged sodas and filling out the spread with a tray piled high with paper-wrapped sandwiches and an oversized basket filled with bags of chips and pretzels.

Lunch was a welcome break and banter went to the football season and prospects for the 49ers.

"There are some pretty amazing cookies over there, so grab one or two, and let's get back to the agenda," Desmond said, finally.

He guided the afternoon agenda fairly well. But by 4:00 energy clearly flagged. While the original intention was to adjourn at 5, he read the room and suggested they wrap up early. "You guys have really given your all, today. And I totally appreciate that. It's that 'all' that's going to make the difference." They seemed relieved and gathered their things.

After picking up the agendas and other printed materials left behind on the table, Jillian walked out of the room with Desmond.

"So?" he asked.

"So I thought it was a major success." *Oh god, somehow she had reverted to her third-grade self, playing to the teacher. And she couldn't stop herself. It felt it too risky to criticize Desmond overtly.* "Yeah, it was good to see everyone working together," she added. "And I keep harping on it, but collaboration is what's going to get us to pull this together. It's our secret weapon."

"Aren't *you* the secret weapon?" he said, teasing.

"Yeah, good point." She purposely changed the subject to her impressions of the hotel and was glad when she parted from Desmond at the BART station entrance, pressed by crowds of commuters but left alone with her thoughts.

CHAPTER 9

O n the train ride back to Berkeley, a loop of dialog between Desmond and Trevor during the meeting played in her head on repeat. Desmond had proposed the company adopt a short list of values: passion, teamwork, communication, fun and service. Jillian thought the list ridiculous and shallow: how were these unique to Sojourner? In any case, Trevor challenged one. Communication.

"We have no insight into the financials of the company," Trevor said. "That does not strike me as real communication. Especially when there are so few of us, and we've all made some real sacrifices to be at Sojourner."

Jillian's gut resonated with what Trevor was saying. At the same time, she cringed at his willingness to challenge Desmond so openly. The rest of the team listened in silence. No one was moving, note-taking and soda sipping stopped. Outside the room, there was the sound of a trolley being pushed along the carpet.

When Desmond paused before answering, Jillian suspected he was trying to swallow his irritation and collect himself. Finally, he said, "I understand why you would say that, Trevor. But I've made a judgment that financials would only be distracting. I'm hoping you will trust me when I say we're doing well. And then get on with your work. It's all about trust and having the depth of character to trust." Desmond folded his hands on the table like a schoolmarm, signaling that the conversation was over.

Trevor cast his eyes to the notebook splayed in front of him. He picked up the pen and began jotting a note, not responding. Desmond moved on, feigning confidence.

Jillian did not feel like moving on, and she felt sorry for Trevor, who she thought was unfairly charged with lacking trust. Sure, she thought companies that proclaimed full transparency and even published employee salaries were naive and childish. But she was curious about how Sojourner was doing and couldn't see how this was a distraction. Westbrook Hotels had long-standing procedures for managing financial information: an annual budgeting process, department financial reports made available to all, and bonuses tied to department and company performance. The financials were shared to motivate and push harder to profit.

Sojourner was also a for-profit company, but it was founded to do good, which felt a bit like a nonprofit. Did that mean there was less pressure on them for revenue? She had not yet heard Desmond comment on revenue. Did revenue not matter at this point in the company's life cycle? Was revenue not something investors cared about, on the backs of legendary loss-ridden tech companies? Sojourner had a dozen hotels in a pilot program in San Francisco already, each of which was paying a small fee. But it would be months before she could grow that number meaningfully enough to have significant revenue.

She put the conversation aside in her head as the train approached her stop. The thought wouldn't emerge again until dinner, when Scott asked her about the meeting.

Jillian described what she termed a "confrontation" between Trevor and Desmond

"Well, I'd hardly call that a confrontation, from the way you described it," Scott said.

"Maybe it wasn't a fistfight, but it was the first time I've heard someone question Desmond. And I thought Trevor had a decent point. Shouldn't we know about revenue or expenses, or at least runway at this point?"

Scott put his fork down. "Not necessarily. You don't need to show a profit for a while. But you do need to manage expenses so you don't run out of cash."

"I guess we need to see the expenses. Or something that shows when we'd hit the end of the runway."

Scott agreed. "Who handles accounting?" he asked.

Desmond once mentioned an accountant, she told him, but never specifics about who this was or how much attention they gave Sojourner.

"See, it's probably well under control, if someone from outside is taking care of the books. And theoretically, your investors should be receiving regular financial reports."

By now, Jillian had also stopped eating and reached for her wine. "I assume so, but I don't know. I've never met our lead investor, and I think there are a number of angel investors involved, too. It's all a little vague how much funding we've received, and how long it'll last."

Scott nodded and bit down on his lower lip. "That's the part I'd be concerned with at this point. Even if you just knew who had oversight on finances besides Desmond. If you knew there was someone else who had visibility, you could rest easier."

"You know, maybe I should talk to Trevor about this. He's been around longer, and he probably knows more."

"Or maybe that's the reason he had the question to begin with: he *doesn't* know more."

Several days later Jillian suggested to Trevor that they get out of the office to review the new product features, where the conversation wouldn't disturb everyone. "Let's meet down at Brew. I have an errand to run first, so I'll just meet you there. See you at 3?" It would be a major improvement when the offices moved to WeWork, with conference rooms to duck into.

Her plan was to start easy. So over her tea and his hot chocolate, Trevor demo'd each of the new features. She genuinely needed the tutorial. Once they got to the end of the list, though, she made her move. He had closed his laptop.

"So," she began. "I've been meaning to ask you about something from the team offsite. The point you made to Desmond about communication. What caused you to bring that up?"

Trevor glanced over his shoulder, which seemed a bit paranoid, but perhaps it was habit. She stared down into her cup, wanting to relieve pressure on him by avoiding eye contact.

"I just, I don't know. Considering how small we are, it just doesn't seem right, how little information we have."

"Desmond seems like he's on the up and up. Is there a reason to distrust?"

Trevor shuffled his feet. "Not necessarily, but then I think you need to earn trust. And to my mind, Desmond has not fully earned that. I've heard him give numbers on the phone that conflict with what he tells us. Mostly around funding and runway. And with every person we hire, we shorten the runway."

"Like me?" she asked, eyebrows raised and with a slight smile.

Trevor laughed. "I guess. Listen, I know we need you, and you've already had a positive impact on the team. But that's what I mean about open communication. How will new hires affect us? This would be reassuring to know." He sighed and looked away, then asked, "Do you have any idea how long before we run out of money? Because I don't."

Jillian shook her head, no. "My son is a VC and he urged me to ask a bunch of questions, but I didn't want to over-inquire. I guess I didn't want to insult Desmond."

"He kind of plays it that way. Like you're questioning him

personally and his integrity. It's not that way at all. I just want to know what's ahead for me. It's about me, not him."

There was something almost childlike about Trevor. He didn't filter his words, and he had expectations about how things should work, which hadn't been worn down by time. She wanted to reassure him, just as she would have Christian. Ironically, though, Trevor and her actual child knew more about startup finances than she did. Recognizing the danger of falling into the role of company mom, she felt herself pulling back.

"Listen," Jillian said finally. "I'm the new kid in town, and Desmond already took a swipe at you during the offsite, so why don't I play it naive with him? Now that I have a better lay of the land and hopefully his trust, I can ask him about this. I think I can be very friendly about it, and not put him on the defensive."

Trevor nodded. She wished he weren't so doe-eyed.

Jillian took out a pen and notebook, and together they reviewed exactly what they wanted to extract from Desmond, in columns labeled "Must Know" and "Nice-to-Know."

"I'm not making any promises on what I'll accomplish, but I'll set up a meeting with him tomorrow and at least we will have tried."

She told him she planned to stay at the coffee shop for another hour to get work done, and watched him walk out. Pulling out her phone, Jillian surveyed Desmond's schedule on their calendar app to find a time to meet.

Funny how things had changed from her first job decades earlier, when calendars were big paper notebooks. Then, you had to literally ask for a meeting by going into your boss's office with your calendar. He (and it was almost always a *he*) would open up his Day-Timer or Week-at-a-Glance, and you'd decide on a time. Now calendars were freely shared online, making it easy to check availability. She even used the calendar as a surveillance tool of sorts, checking where Desmond claimed to be when he disappeared from the office for long stretches. It didn't even feel wrong to check. He probably did the same with all of them.

Jillian created an event on her calendar titled "Catch Up" for the following day, added Desmond as an attendee, and hit "send invitation." She would hope for the best.

CHAPTER 10

J illian knew it wasn't fair to ambush Desmond about the financials, but it seemed the only way to have a face-to-face conversation about it. He met up with her at Brew, cheerful and assuming it was an innocent check-in, sipping his latte as Adele crooned mournfully in the background. So now, as she told him that employee morale was waning because people didn't know how the company was doing financially, his face fell.

"Listen, I have no problem showing you the numbers," he said. "*You* get it. But I have no intention of letting a bunch of developers who have never seen a P&L before dissect them." Desmond fidgeted in his chair and rolled up his sleeves. The room was not warm.

He made a reasonable point, she thought, but he missed something. "I understand, but it's not black or white. You don't have to take *off* the kimono, just open it enough for everyone to feel like they have a comfort level with the financial plan." The kimono metaphor invoked an uncomfortable image, so she stopped there.

"So how would I do that?"

Jillian was surprised he didn't get it. Obviously, Desmond could have a meeting where he presented top-line numbers and a plan. She reminded herself of the goal: for him to take some action, not for her to prove him wrong. She described the 30,000-foot report he could give, then added, "And I'll take you up on the offer for me to take a look at the details. I don't claim to be an accountant, but I just know sometimes it's helpful for someone else to offer a different perspective. Plus a shoulder to cry on or someone to celebrate with." She wanted to be reassuring.

He stared at his coffee mug. Finally, he looked her in the eye. "Okay, I'll share the file when I get back to the office. And why don't you schedule a team meeting for next week and I'll pull together something for everyone."

"Want my help in planning that meeting?"

"Thanks, but I've got this."

She hated the phrase, "I've got this," a response Christian tended to use when she tried to offer him something—food, money, help. It implied an indignant cockiness at being questioned and always seemed to be aimed at shutting down the conversation.

As Desmond left the coffee shop, she actually grinned. Yes, what Desmond was doing brought up all sorts of conflicting emotions. Distrust and hope at the same time. But she finally had someone to commiserate with, someone who knew Desmond well and shared her concerns. An ally. She picked up her phone and messaged Trevor. *Desmond agreed to a team meeting to share top-line financials.* Trevor responded with a fingers-crossed emoji. Jillian didn't tell him Desmond was giving *her* access to the files, full financial disclosure. Why call attention to her unearned status within the company?

She pulled up the calendar, entered a time block, and sent invites to the team meeting, with the title "Sojourner Financial Overview." She figured the meeting had about an 80 percent chance of actually happening, based on Desmond's sketchy record of showing up for all-hands meetings. And if it did happen, there was only a 30 percent chance of the meeting being a success, based on Desmond's natural inclination to elude. Still, if it failed, it would be 100 percent on

Desmond. She had done what she could.

Two days passed. Desmond had not shared the file. Jillian sent a message, carefully crafted as a casual reminder. She'd known this would happen. When the file actually showed up in a Slack direct message that night, she was almost disappointed. Maybe his intentions were solid after all.

Her phone on the kitchen counter and a glass of wine in hand, Jillian was anxious to be able to talk about work with someone she knew she could trust for an honest, knowledgeable opinion. Which is why she'd sent Christian the financials file to look over. She clicked on the Facetime icon, and his face appeared on the screen.

"Hi, Christian, I know it's late there and you must be beat. Did you get the file?"

Christian nodded. He had propped several pillows behind his back to sit upright on the hotel room bed. "I'm actually less tired than I expected, but I'm still on California time. New York will catch up with me tomorrow morning. And yes, I got the file but I haven't had a chance to look at it. Hold on a sec."

Jillian took a sip of wine, a nervous tick. She watched Christian's face, searching for positive or negative interpretation. Any kind of clue.

"It's not out of the ordinary," he said finally.

She exhaled. "Thank God. The last thing I need is to have Sojourner flame out my first month."

"One thing is odd, though. What I'm seeing here isn't reflective of what he showed when he pitched us. Of course, that was a couple months ago and things could have changed. Or he may not have used real numbers in the pitch deck."

"I've been at investor meetings, and I know for a fact his pitch numbers are not real."

Christian adjusted his posture on the bed. "Okay, that is forgivable, to a point. As long as it's not because he's trying to hide something. The other thing is that you're basically out of money, which may be why he's ramped up measures to get funding immediately. Also, the salaries line item seems high for the size of the company."

"So what does that mean?" she asked.

"Overspending on staffing. It could be that salaries are over-market. Does that seem plausible?"

She laughed, almost a sneer. "Not based on my own. Plus, he's a ruthless negotiator."

"Well, there could be people offshore or contracted that you're not aware of."

"Again, not likely. I would have heard something in that small room of an office. I don't see any work coming in except by those I know."

"Actually, the most salient data point is that it looks like you'll burn through your cash in about a month. So that means he's going to have to lock down a raise pretty damn soon. That's pretty tight timing, even in the best-case scenario.

He continued, "I guess the question is, how are you going to discuss this with him? You said he was reluctant to even share this. And I can see why."

There was no good answer. She knew she'd need to be an ally to Desmond, so he wouldn't get defensive and close her out. She asked Christian for his advice.

"Well, you could start the conversation with the salaries situation and ask for detail with an excuse: you want to plan your own department's future staffing. That makes sense, right? Eventually, you would be hiring sales or marketing staff?"

"Well, eventually." She jotted a note in her Moleskin but was doubtful that would work.

Christian continued. "On the runway side of things, you could say you wanted to help him more with fundraising, that the two of you could conceivably raise faster than he could alone. Then you'd have more insight into exactly what his prospects were of closing a round asap."

"I went with him to one investor meeting. He hardly gave me a chance to speak, and when I questioned some numbers from the deck, he basically said, 'That's what founders do,' and shut me down."

Christian laughed. "Yeah, it kind of *is* what founders do. But the numbers have to have some truth to them, otherwise, in doing due diligence, the investor will see the gap and turn Sojourner down. Do you know what kind of response he's gotten so far?"

She sighed and explained that based on the number of meetings that were on his calendar, with no positive results, things weren't going well. "Seems like at every team meeting, he's giving good news about someone he just met who was very interested. But then, nothing."

"So either he's misreporting that, or they *are* interested...until they dig further. Have you asked if he's gotten any feedback from the *no's*?"

"I haven't. It's a good idea. Ultimately, my goal should be to fix the financial health of Sojourner, not to indict him. Figuratively speaking, of course."

Christian nodded. "Right. I'd love to see my mom take down a company, though. It's every kid's family hero fantasy, right?"

"Right. And I suspect having an unemployed mother—again—is not part of that fantasy," she said. "Listen, thanks for looking at the file. I'll need to figure out how to handle this. And you get some sleep. Jet lag can cripple you."

After hanging up, she lingered there at the counter, finishing her wine and wondering how she could confront Desmond *without* confronting him. What she really wanted was for her concerns to go away. She wanted to know the company was thriving, so she could focus on the reason she took the job.

Scott walked in from the garage, wiping his hands with a rag. "Hey, gorgeous. Why the long face?"

Was it that obvious? "How would you feel if one of your employees asked about the store's finances?"

"Pissed."

As she feared.

Jillian punched his arm with a fake blow. "I was just talking to Christian, and I showed him Sojourner's P&L."

She relayed the gist of the conversation. "So I've likely already pissed Desmond off." What she couldn't get herself to say was that she had also betrayed his confidence in a way, by showing the P&L to an investor. Even if it was Christian. "So how do I get more involved without turning Desmond off? Even if there's no impropriety or problem, Desmond is not going to respond well if I question him about it. Your answer is proof of that."

Scott wiped his hands one last time and threw the rag onto the counter. "Okay, well, I know your intentions are generous. But he doesn't know that. So I guess step one is to build trust. He needs to know that you're in it for all the right reasons. That you won't betray him."

Jillian's face tightened.

"Do you think he'd be up for meeting us for dinner?" Scott asked. "Is he married? Sometimes getting together outside work cements the relationship."

Dear, dear Scott. He always knew the right thing to do.

"That's perfect. And yes, he's married. I know very little about his wife. No kids. I'll see if they can meet us at a restaurant in the city next weekend. Or the next. From what he says, they have a fairly active social life."

"Unlike these two empty-nesters?"

She laughed. "Hey, give us a break. We went to the Spiderman movie last week. That counts." Jillian's passion for Marvel films bucked the demographic.

"If you say so. And since we have a boring evening at home tonight, we might as well make the best of it. Why don't you pour yourself another glass and one for me, and I'll make dinner. How about chicken fried rice, my go-to leftover-cleanup dish?"

She nodded and opened the refrigerator to pull out a carton of eggs, some leftover chicken, two-day-old rice, and a bag of frozen peas and carrots.

Jillian couldn't shake a dark, almost self-righteous thought: to uncover something amiss at Sojourner would be satisfying in a weird way. As Christian had described: to be the hero, when Desmond wasn't. She pushed that aside, ashamed. She wanted to be better than that, to only have the company's best interests at heart. The wine splashed into Scott's glass, she twisted the bottle, then filled her own glass.

CHAPTER 11

As they waited for the maître d' to appear, Anna announced that this was one of her favorite restaurants, The four of them were huddled against the biting air by the door, which opened intermittently for patrons leaving or entering, each time squeezing them farther to the side of the small and crowded lobby.

Thank goodness. Jillian had spent way too much time selecting the restaurant, over-searching OpenTable, Yelp and Eater, hoping for Desmond and Anna's approval yet unsure about their taste. The couple operated at a higher level of hip than she and Scott, and being childless in their thirties, Jillian imagined they ate out a lot. Slanted Door seemed safe. It was well regarded and well located—looking out on the bay in the Ferry Building. While it wasn't Jillian's personal favorite, it was the kind of restaurant one couldn't *dislike,* she rationalized. She was relieved it hit the mark with Anna.

She was not at all what Jillian had pictured, whatever that was. Physically, Anna was imposing—almost as tall as Desmond. With black hair cut sleek in an updated bob, very pale skin that charcoal eye shadow emphasized, and cherry-red lips—it all projected celebrity-style confidence. Both she and Desmond were dressed in simple clothes—a little black dress for Anna and black cashmere crewneck with dark jeans for Desmond. Jillian sized up both outfits as expensive, with refined details like subtle topstitching and perfect tailoring. Somehow the look bound them together as a couple. Jillian remembered the days when she and Scott relished getting dressed for date night, wanting to achieve a certain look, acutely aware of how that look reflected on them as a couple. Lately, they felt satisfied with a quick "you look nice" for each other before going out the door. Which was enough.

On the drive to the restaurant, Jillian announced to Scott that her goal for the evening was to assess Desmond's trustworthiness.

Scott laughed. "I thought we talked about the purpose being to build trust between you two. I thought you wanted Desmond to feel more comfortable pulling you into the financial conversations and fundraising. Now the evening seems more like a secret lie detector test."

"Oh, right. You kind of busted me there." She was glad he couldn't see her face from the driver's seat. "I forgot about that. I like your more constructive approach. As opposed to my cross-examination." She smiled, glancing over at him.

"You're overthinking this, Jillian. I mean, going into a nice dinner at a lovely restaurant with a stated goal? Really? Have you set any OKRs?" Scott tossed his head back a little, satisfied that he'd thrown in the acronym for Objectives and Key Results as if he were a startup guy. Plus, he knew just how to tease her into seeing her own ridiculousness without getting defensive.

"Yeah, I'll show you my PowerPoint once we're parked," she joked. But his point was well taken. *Loosen up. This is hardly national diplomacy here. Enjoy a good meal with nice people.*

The foursome was led to a table by the floor-to-ceiling windows, the lights of the Bay Bridge casting a magical glow on the table. There was a little shuffle, some hesitation, about who should sit where. Finally, after chairs scraped on the polished concrete and they settled, each fussed a little—Desmond fingering the chopsticks, Jillian arranging the silverware more precisely, and Anna following the lights of a ferry steering into its berth. Scott picked at a piece of lint on his jacket.

"Desmond told me you're in sales, Anna. What kind of company?" Jillian smiled as she said it, wanting the conversation to sound effortless, unrehearsed.

"I lead a team that sells Oracle consulting services."

What did that mean? If she was going to keep Anna talking, she'd need to ask some questions. Even if she sounded stupid. "Um, Oracle is business software, right? So how does that work if you don't work for Oracle? I guess I need your version of Oracle for Dummies."

"Totally reasonable if you're not in the business." Anna smiled in a way that may have been patronizing; Jillian wasn't sure. "Companies usually need the Oracle software customized so they can set it up for their particular business. That's where we come in." She described how they helped one of their long-standing clients, a chocolate manufacturer. "So that's it in a nutshell. It's not as sexy as working at a startup, but I enjoy it."

Desmond and Jillian exchanged amused glances. Desmond said, "*Sexy* is hardly the adjective I'd use to describe a startup. What do you think, Jillian? You're new to the game so have a clearer perspective."

She laughed. "It's messy working at a startup. I mean, that's not specific to Sojourner. It's the nature of a new company. So I would definitely decline the *sexy* adjective." She talked about coming from a well-established company and how it differed from startup life. "In my old job, I was improving time-tested processes and ideas. Now I find myself inventing everything from scratch. And the whole point is to get away from doing what's already being done. That's what disruption is all about, right? So there's going to be a lot of messiness and missteps, by definition." She wanted to make some comment about her age but held back lest it call attention to the gap between the two couples.

The server came by, introduced himself, and was turned away by Scott as they picked up their menus for the first time. They chattered about the food, discussed which dishes were favorites, and agreed to share two appetizers to start. When Scott wondered out loud about *rau ram* and *shaking beef*, Desmond and Anna answered with authority. Jillian felt a little small-town.

She let the others carry the conversation a while, trying to relax. Luckily, Desmond now had a lot of questions for Scott about On the Board, and Scott was obviously flattered by the interest.

"You're really a startup," Desmond said. "Just the old-fashioned way, doing it without venture capital, or at least I presume. Do you have plans to scale? I mean, to expand? See, I'm guilty of seeing all business through the startup lens."

Scott laughed. No, he didn't want to expand. He wanted the one store to be as profitable as possible, and for it to continue to support them well. "It's also important to me to take care of my employees. I really care about these kids. And I call them kids because they're mostly in their 20s, the same age as my own kid. For a couple of them, their fathers either died or were derelicts, and I'm kind of their father figure. So I consider the store a place for them to grow and mature, and hopefully get some skills."

"What'll happen to the store when you retire? Does Christian want to be involved?"

Scott and Jillian both laughed. "Hell no," Scott said. "He sees much grander things ahead."

Desmond turned to Anna. "Christian is a VC. In fact, that's how I met Jillian. I pitched Pier 45 Capital, and Christian couldn't make the investment but thought Jillian and Sojourner might be a good fit."

Jillian was surprised Anna didn't already know this.

"Wow, Christian must be doing all right for himself if he's a VC at his age, making the big bucks," Anna said.

"Yes and no. He's just a glorified lackey at this point. But he's loving it, and it'll no doubt lead to some interesting opportunities."

"Well, it sounds like he has the right idea. Follow the money."

Jillian didn't know about that, but she was glad Christian was so self-directed. When she was his age, she had a liberal arts degree behind her and was answering phones at a hotel to pay the rent, with no idea what she wanted to do with her life. It had all turned out fine, but she admired that Christian was very intentional in his career, without being the ugly kind of ambitious. He was actually quite grounded and kind. Which ultimately, is a mother's best brag, she thought.

Anna glanced around the room furtively, then excused herself to find the restroom.

The conversation moved to Sojourner, and Scott asked Desmond a number of very pointed questions. His possibly-offensive directness was masked by an apparent naivete Jillian knew to be manufactured.

"So, where are you guys in raising Series A?"

Desmond shifted his weight and cleared his throat. "The bar has gotten really high for Series A lately, it's crazy. VCs mostly won't buy in before you have some substantial MRR. That's monthly recurring revenue. So we'll probably be doing another seed round."

"Is there a deadline…or, I'm not sure what you call it. In my business, we just call it running out of money. Cash flow." Scott said it with a naivete that Jillian knew was not pure.

Desmond's smile was forced. "We're fine."

Jillian bristled at the platitude, then used it as an opening.

"You know, Desmond, I did a lot of budget management stuff at Westbrook. I'd be happy to sit with you and work through the P&L line-by-line."

Scott jumped in. "Honey, speaking as a CEO, that can be uncomfortable." He was playing this perfectly, Jillian thought. "I did that with Jackson, my right-hand guy. Under duress, I might add. He wouldn't stop badgering me about it. But it turns out, even though he was 21 at the time, he asked some damn good questions. Actually, fast forward five years and he's lined up to buy the business when I retire since Christian is otherwise occupied. Ultimately, I'd have to say I found it helpful to have someone to run the financial stuff past."

"We'll see," Desmond said, rescued by the arrival of plates of barbecued pork ribs and vegetarian dumplings. Anna returned to the table with what seemed to be new energy, practically squealing in delight at the food in front of them.

The conversation never returned to Sojourner, and Jillian was okay with that. The goal was just to establish rapport, she reminded herself, and that was better done with other topics. All in all, it was a pleasant evening.

As Jillian and Scott waited for the restaurant valet to bring their car around, they shivered in the cold wind off the bay. She glanced over her shoulder to be sure Desmond and Anna had actually gotten into their Uber. Then she edged even closer to Scott. "So?"

"So, what?"

"Did I meet my goal?"

"Oh my god, you're incredible," he said, shaking his head in disbelief, but smiling.

She knew him well enough to know that wasn't a compliment, but instead commentary on her dogged pursuit of the goal. She raised her eyebrows to show she got the dig but wasn't buying it.

"Well, I guess, yes. I think we had a pleasant evening together and I don't know how he *couldn't* trust you, now that he knows you have a weakness for artisan cotton candy and will fight to the nail to grab it for yourself from the supposedly *shared* Confections Assortment Plate."

"Was that out of line?" She didn't wait for an answer. "So yes, I guess just knowing each other better helps everything. Thanks, by the way, for being the perfect plant, directing the conversation to funding, runway, and all that."

"It's an honor to play for Team Johnson," he said.

"Okay, well, don't forget, I'm the team captain."

"Yeah, well, I'm the team manager."

As the car pulled up, Scott left her side to tip the valet and slide into the driver's seat. On the other side of the car, Jillian got the door open and was seated before the valet could get to her, but he managed to slam the door shut after checking that her legs were indeed tucked in.

"What did you think of Anna?" she asked.

"There's nothing to dislike. Attractive. Sexy in an exotic way. A bit intimidating. Clearly likes to be the center of things. Tons of energy. Maybe too much. But all that fits for sales. She seems pretty successful in her own right."

"I'll need to check her LinkedIn profile. Heck, I think I'll connect with her there. I did think she was a tad snobby. She knew almost too much about the food. And the wine. Did you catch that she basically told Desmond which bottle to order?"

"Desmond is the head of the family, and Anna is the neck that turns the head," Scott said. "Old Polish saying."

Jillian laughed. "Do we have a two-headed family?"

"Maybe so. I'm damn glad that we make decisions together. And I'll be sure to let you know if you're bossing me around."

"And vice versa."

They sped across the Bay Bridge and along the freeway through Berkeley, then poked through a few stoplights before gliding into their driveway. The easy return to their quiet bungalow was payoff for a dinner that was pleasant enough, but one they were both happy to have behind them.

CHAPTER 12

As her phone alarm buzzed and she opened her eyes, a shadow crept over Jillian. It was moving day for Sojourner. She hit snooze but couldn't fall back to sleep.

Jillian considered herself organized by nature, but on days like this she was less smug about it. Even twenty years ago, organizing this move would have been no big deal. She'd want to shine for her boss and would work like crazy to get all the details right. Now, though, she had more experience and knew that all sorts of impossible-to-anticipate things could go wrong. She'd supervised many an upheaval in the last ten years, and it was always the unexpected that took you down. The person who doesn't show up. The key locked inside the truck. The landlord whose mother died and forgot to reserve the elevator for you.

Finally, she gave in to the alarm and jumped out of bed, determined to be the first one to the office. She'd asked everyone else to show up by 9, which didn't happen on a regular basis. But even these night-owl developers could get there by 9 if required, she rationalized. *Grow up, guys. This is how the real world works.*

Admittedly, this would be a DIY operation, more like a college student move than a business move. And she was okay with that because it seemed in keeping with their scrappy, early-stage status. Trevor had volunteered his mother's old minivan so they wouldn't need to rent a truck. Their one extravagance was some boxes she purchased at Staples, along with packing tape. While WeWork was walkable from their current office, only five blocks, they had an assortment of computers and monitors that would go in the minivan, plus the usual collection of office junk they wouldn't be able to move without boxing.

The trickiest part of the operation was coordinating use of both buildings' service elevators. In the hours she spent negotiating with the building managers to coordinate reservation times, Jillian consumed almost a full roll of Tums. But in the end, she got what she wanted—an hour at the old building followed by an hour at the new building. She scheduled it tightly, but it was better that way. Contain the pain, as Scott liked to say.

At 9:05 Jillian glanced at her watch, alone in the office. Even Desmond had not taken her 9 a.m. request seriously. Trevor texted to say he'd have the van by the front door at 9:30 sharp. She'd need to get everything into the elevator starting at 9:15, and packing needed to happen first.

Damn it, am I the only adult in the room? It was just a saying, but it was almost literally true for her at the company. Though ironic, since she actually was the *only* person in the room at the moment. She taped up a box and began piling into it the detritus on desks. If they didn't show up on time, they lost their right to have their stuff packed carefully or in a labeled box.

At 9:20 everyone arrived at once. Jillian looked at her watch, a gesture not missed by Desmond. He shouldered the rebuff for all as he claimed they'd waited "forever" for an elevator. She didn't even bother to hide her aggravation as she barked instructions. Thankfully, now they had the bodies she'd need to load the service elevator, babysit it on the ground floor in case Trevor hadn't yet arrived, and then load everything into the van. She estimated they'd need just two elevator runs to handle everything. Then reverse and repeat once Trevor ferried the boxes to WeWork. The crew would walk over, but considering Trevor would be poking along in traffic and would need to find a place to park or at least pull over, they very well may beat him.

What could have gone wrong with any number of miscues, instead was a perfectly timed dance. Even with the rocky start, the elevator orchestration worked out. Jillian was quite pleased with herself. By noon, the move was complete. Desks had been selected, computers and monitors had been set up, knickknacks were restored to their rightful owners, and they ordered pizza to celebrate, a rare splurge.

The new office was no larger than the previous one, but it was classier. That startup cachet, along with the conference rooms and kitchen facilities, was behind Desmond's desire to move to WeWork, Jillian speculated. Two large windows looked onto Market Street, and the remaining three walls were all glass. A decal of Sojourner's logo at eye-level on the glass sliding door to the hall was a nice touch, an upgrade. Jillian was amused that the glass on the side walls was blackened to waist height, to provide privacy she supposed. Back in the day, you sat at an actual desk, with drawers, and the desks used to have what they called a privacy panel in the front so no one could see up your skirt. Now they worked at long tables, which they called desks, but weren't. They were small, staked-out territories with dedicated chairs.

Jillian selected one of the two seats by the windows. Desmond claimed the other. At first, she cringed inside, thinking that sitting side-by-side with the CEO would be restricting. Then she realized it may actually play to her advantage. In the old office, he sat in a niche of sorts with a door he closed for private calls, like with investors. Perhaps here she would overhear more of his conversations, learn some things. At the same time, she remembered that throughout WeWork were numerous banks of phone booths, created for just that reason: to have private conversations in the open office world. Maybe he'd make his phone calls in the booths. How she missed the old days of private offices. Even cubicles now were a luxury.

The all-hands meeting Desmond promised, where he would review the company financials, had not happened. On the morning for which it was scheduled, Desmond sent a Slack message: *Sorry, guys. We'll need to defer today's team meeting. An investor meeting just came up.* He added, *#priorities.* The hashtag didn't do much to assuage Jillian's irritation. On the other hand, she felt a twisted sense of superiority. She predicted exactly this, and it reaffirmed a lack of trust that was brewing for her, despite the dinner at Slanted Door.

Desmond had finally rescheduled the meeting, after dogged follow-up by Jillian. The timing was odd—the afternoon of moving day—but maybe that was just as well, she thought. The team gathered down the hall in a conference room labeled with a three-foot *B* painted on the glass wall.

"How cool is this to be talking about the State of Sojourner in…drumroll…an actual conference room?" Desmond said, to open the meeting. The faces around the room showed they were feeling it, too, and Jillian was begrudgingly glad for Desmond. She knew he did not want to hold the meeting. A happy vibe, one that they were making progress, would buoy him.

Jillian knew in her bones that Desmond would not reveal any new information. That was just how he rolled. She also knew his strength was getting people to feel good. Well, maybe that was half the battle, she thought as he put a slide deck up on the large screen that dominated one wall. This would be a pep talk.

She was not wrong.

Trevor Slacked Jillian at the end of the day: *Quick drink?*

They met downstairs in the building lobby at 5 o'clock, making a point of not leaving the office together. It was like they were having an affair but they were cheating on Desmond, Jillian thought as the elevator reached the first floor and she saw Trevor waiting for her.

"Where to?" she asked him, voice chipper.

A new office, even if just five blocks away, meant resetting every habit, including the standard venue to meet for drinks. After a couple minutes throwing out ideas and a quick check of Yelp, they headed to the lobby of the Victory Hotel. Ironically, it was a throwback to where they had held the team offsite and Trevor and Jillian had their first conversation about frustrations with Sojourner.

They found a small table in the corner of the bar tucked off the lobby, a room so dark and dripping in black that it felt almost sinister, even with the few touches of neon. The server appeared surprisingly quickly, slapping cocktail napkins down in front of each. Trevor quizzed him on the subtleties between various IPAs before settling on one with a funny name. Jillian ordered a Dewar's on the rocks, so straightforward, then wondered whether Trevor would deem Scotch as something his mother with the beat-up minivan would order.

"So?" Jillian had resolved not to succumb to the millennial habit of starting sentences with *so*, but it was the perfect start to a conversation like this, the opening to a chapter, not a sentence. And to not state the topic, to imply that he knew, underscored that she and Trevor had a bond, a secretive mission they shared.

"Yeah, well, it was *nice*. The meeting was nice," he said. "That's all: *nice*."

Jillian raised her eyebrows.

"It painted a rosy picture. No surprise there. But it didn't answer my main questions. Which are…. One: Exactly where we are on raising funds? Who's committed and what are the critical dates and the near-term plan, and how does all that affect our runway? And, two: "How will new hires affect the bottom line?"

Jillian had always appreciated people who spoke as if writing, and the ability to number points for the listener was high on her list of virtues. Plus, Trevor had not been distracted by the overly optimistic red herrings in the PowerPoint, able to see what was missing.

"You're 100 percent right," she said, feeling a little guilty that she was not telling Trevor she had seen the actual P&L. Anyway, she had the exact same questions he did. "What do you think the other developers made of it? Any Slack side-chatter?"

From what he could tell, the others didn't seem to care. "I'm tired of this shit. I'm just going to ask him."

"What makes you think you're going to get a straight answer, even one-on-one?"

He just shrugged.

"Do you know the accountant?" Jillian asked.

"No, but her name is Julie Strauss. Desmond's not the greatest at hiding things on his calendar. Why?"

"Scott suggested this. Maybe there's a way you could reach out to her and ask just the right questions to get better insight, the actual numbers."

"Wouldn't she say I should ask Desmond?"

"Not if you're really clever about why you say you need to know. You could say he asked you to work out a few things for him. You're such a nice guy, I have no doubt you'd be able to win her trust."

"Wow. White lies?" Trevor had a twinkle in his eye. "From you, who I thought was straight as an arrow."

She laughed. "I am. But when there's a good cause, sometimes you need to get a little creative. Our intention is to help, not harm. And most likely there's no reason to believe any impropriety is going on so who cares, really, if we see the numbers?" What she didn't say, was that she'd have a hard time bluffing her way through a conversation like that—even when it was justified. Which is why she'd put it on him.

The server arrived with the drinks and a small bowl of warm mixed nuts. The Victory just earned permanent after-works-drinks status in Jillian's mind. She could get over the Goth vibe for warm mixed nuts.

"We could have stayed at WeWork and had a beer," Trevor said. "For free."

"Yeah, but there we couldn't scheme to find our Deep Throat. We needed the cover of a dark bar."

"Deep Throat?"

Was he...blushing? Jillian did a quick calculation. Trevor wasn't even alive for Watergate. But oh, no! He most likely thought of the reference as porn. Now she was blushing, too. She dug deep for some indignation. "Watergate? Woodward and Bernstein's informant? All the President's Men? Stream it on Netflix."

They clicked their glasses to confirm co-conspiracy and began to brainstorm scripts Trevor could use with Julie Strauss.

CHAPTER 13

A ringing phone before 10 a.m. is never good. Today was no exception.

"Honey, do you think you can come with us to hear the results of your father's cognitive status testing with Dr. Williamson on Thursday?"

Jillian sank into the plush chair in the kitchen sitting area. Everything else, and now this?

"What time is it scheduled for, Mom?"

As her mother spoke, Jillian silently scrambled to create a plan to dodge this gracefully. Yes, she knew it was better for her parents to have another set of ears. And she should probably hear the results first-hand, since as an only child, this could have a serious impact on her life. But the two-hour drive to Grass Valley would slice a wide swath from her workday. Double it to include the two-hour drive back, maybe longer with afternoon traffic. She had a smattering of hotel calls lined up on Thursday. It would mean rescheduling four of them. She calculated that maybe she could keep her 9 a.m. call and leave for Grass Valley immediately after.

"I know it's a bother, honey," her mother said, offering a veiled apology when Jillian had not jumped in to say *yes*.

"It's not a bother, Mom." This seemed the only response, and she consciously made it sound sincere. "I'm just checking my calendar. Do you think the doctor would agree to Facetiming me in? That way I could save some serious drive time."

"How would that work? Do doctors do that? Well, I suppose I could ask him."

Jillian knew she was being selfish. She imagined her mother ruminating after they'd hang up about how to ask the doctor for this. She hated rattling her mother. "No, actually. I'd be happy to come. It's always valuable to have an extra perspective on an evaluation. And I'm curious about the results. So count me in."

"Oh, you're the best, honey." They arranged to meet at her parents' home and drive together to the medical offices. When Jillian hung up, she felt slightly satisfied that she'd done the right thing and pushed aside distress at the work it would take to reschedule her appointments. *#Priorities*, she told herself mimicking Desmond, but she was only partway in on that sentiment.

A Slack notification popped up. From Trevor. "Just spoke with Julie Strauss. Can I grab a phone booth and call you?"

"Really?" she said out loud. There were too many things coming at her today, and it was still early. Too early. And what was Trevor doing at work before 10?

"Sure. Benefit of working from home: no phone booth needed for me. Call me when you're ready."

Ten minutes later she glanced at her watch. She wondered whether Trevor had gotten caught in a situation where he couldn't leave the office after all. Just then, the phone rang.

"Sorry. The phone booth situation at WeWork is crazy. People are camped out in them, eating breakfast? I don't know. Working? Doing all sorts of things that are not phone calls. I tried four different floors before I found one that was free."

"Sucks," Jillian said. She was starting to sound like a 25-year-old. "That goes to show you, people are desperate for privacy. The era of group work is over. Bring back private offices."

"I wish. Anyway, I did my best with the accountant, but I'm not sure I made any progress."

Trevor had bluffed his way through an excuse for the call. He said he had some investment opportunities coming up and wanted to figure out if he should exercise some Sojourner options instead. Even though she wasn't really the person who would have that information or insight, it gave him a reason to start the call.

"She didn't seem to indicate that there was anything untoward going on. Or anything that worried her. And it seemed like she was fairly hands-on with financial review, taxes, and all that. I probed a bit on the salary expense, and she didn't bite. All in all, it was kind of a dead end."

"I suppose. But if nothing else, it's one lead or avenue we can cross off the list. And it gives me some comfort to know that a third party has some oversight. I think it's her job...isn't it in some accounting code of conduct or something...to raise any red flags?"

"Maybe. But think of all the accountants at Enron. Or Wells Fargo. All sorts of bad stuff can go on without catching the watchdogs' attention."

On the corner of her screen, Jillian saw an email notification from her mother with the subject line, "Dad's appointment details." She slouched further and turned her attention back to Trevor without opening it.

"Okay, so what's next?" She hoped Trevor had the answer.

"I'm stumped. Business as usual? Head down and hope for the best?"

She couldn't believe Trevor was saying this. Wasn't the millennial generation motivated by principles and making the world a better place? Maybe so, but realistically, they were at a dead end. And she was a Baby Boomer, even if at the tail end of it. They were the generation that solved everything by working harder.

"Trevor, you're an old soul," she said, knowing he'd have no idea what she meant.

"Okay?" he said, leaving that hanging. Then, "See you in the office later this week?"

When they hung up, she sat a few minutes in that big comfy chair, staring out the window at a squirrel that was poised on a branch of the big coastal oak that dominated their backyard. His pause would not last but a moment, she knew. In a heartbeat he'd scamper up to chase one of his yard kin. She listened to her own breath. And as soon as he vanished from sight, the faint sound of his claws on the bark fell from memory, too. She pulled up the calendar app on her phone and began to strategize about how to reschedule those appointments.

Four days later, Jillian sat in traffic on I80 just outside Sacramento, tapping the steering wheel, anxious to get home. Not even Bruce Springsteen turned up loud in the car had raised her mood. It would be a long slog back to Berkeley if this jam-up were any indication. Her mother clearly wasn't happy she'd declined the offer to go out to lunch, but Jillian was preoccupied with getting back to the safe haven of home, where her life was under her control. Or at least she could process everything alone or with Scott. There had been a lot to take in.

The appointment with Dr. Williamson had been efficient. She had to hand it to him for that. He had clearly learned to balance just the right amount of information, with enough compassion to allow the patient and family to get through the appointment. Their grief would come later. But the doctor couldn't have that in his office.

As they all took seats around a polished cherry table, the doctor thanked Jillian in particular for coming. "It's helpful to have another family member here," he said. Which she knew meant the news was not good. In return, her rote, "Happy to," was hollow.

He opened a manila folder with a small stack of copies within and passed them across the table to the three of them. "These tests give us a lot of information." He turned to Jillian and explained, "Part of the assessment is written, but much of it involves a series of questions, a conversation really, with a specialist. So it's a thorough evaluation."

"Questions like who's the president? Isn't that sort of obvious?"

"No. While that's one of the standard questions, the bulk of it actually tests short-term memory, which tends to be what is lost first. So for example, we'll ask the patient to commit to memory some information, like a person's address, or to read aloud a paragraph. We test the immediate recall. Then later in the interview, we ask the patient to recall that information again."

"I'm not sure I could pass that myself," Jillian joked. They all laughed, including Dr. Williamson, but they all knew it wasn't true. The joke was actually meant to cut through the tension in the room.

At the top of the report was a summary of results, and Dr. Williamson reviewed this, line by line. Jillian's father had scored under the 50th percentile for all dimensions, and the report concluded, underlined: MILD TO MODERATE COGNITIVE IMPAIRMENT.

"I can't conclusively say this indicates Alzheimer's Disease, because the only way to diagnose conclusively is highly invasive—such as through an autopsy." He smiled.

Her parents laughed nervously. Jillian could not even smile. That joke was cruel.

Driving back to her parents' house, they only lightly skirted the topic of the meeting.

"I guess I'm officially getting forgetful," her father had said, with a casualness like, "I'm undeniably over-the-hill," which he announced every birthday lately.

Before Jillian climbed into her own car, she hugged both and said over her shoulder, "Mom, I'll call you tonight and we can go over the recommendations." Already she dreaded the call, strapping on her seat belt.

The stop-and-go progress through Sacramento finally broke, and Jillian sailed along for at least 20 minutes before she saw brake lights ahead. Her dark thoughts were broken by the phone ringing. Christian. Perfect.

"Hi, honey. Everything okay?"

"Thanks for the vote of confidence. Of course everything's okay."

"You'll understand once you have your first child. Anyway, what's up?"

"Just checking in. You said you were going up to Grass Valley and I wondered what the doc said."

She hesitated. Here was her baby, asking about her father's dementia. How could any of this be? Time was warped and uneven and was tripping her up. "I'm driving home now. It was Okay. I mean it wasn't. Oh, I don't know. The straight-up news is that the report showed mild to moderate dementia. The doctor said he thought it was Alzheimer's but couldn't be 100 percent sure. It could be small strokes. And they're checking him for any possible vitamin deficiencies. The fact is, he's losing his memory."

"Oh god."

"Exactly."

"Does he seem different to you?"

"Not really. Overall. I'm not sure you'd notice a big difference."

"He doesn't come to the phone anymore."

"Right. But otherwise?" She stopped a second to think. "I mean, he repeats himself now and again. But don't we all? Is that really enough to be an Alzheimer's diagnosis?"

"Data doesn't lie."

"It's not exactly quantitative data—more, qualitative. And open to quite a bit of interpretation."

"Including us interpreting that the diagnosis is wrong, even if it's not."

"True. The fact is, they're putting him on a couple drugs that may slow the progress. An insurance policy, I think. Though from what I read recently, it's looking like the drugs don't actually work."

"Well, placebos are of value."

He had a point, so she changed the subject. "Hey, I meant to tell you that Trevor spoke with the Sojourner accountant, which was a dead end. Also, I'm going with Desmond to an investor meeting on Monday - Ian Sondquist."

"Ian is good. No BS tolerated. He won't let Desmond off the hook. So that may be instructive."

"Oh great. That means he won't let me off the hook either."

"You wanted to be in the game; these are the rules of engagement. Call me after."

The traffic now was at a complete standstill. Then stop-and-go. So Jillian stewed as she tapped on the gas when the creeping pace picked up, then shifted her foot back from the pedal when it stopped, as she imagined all the questions Sondquist could nail her on. Offered up for the kill.

CHAPTER 14

I an Sondquist read from the bar chart on the giant screen that covered most of the conference room wall.

"Are your revenue numbers actual?" he asked.

Desmond's slides, with a deep purple, blue and green palate, were A+ in design, mesmerizing in their simple elegance. Was it purposeful that the VC didn't move his glance to Desmond when he asked?

Jillian had heard revenue numbers quoted off-the-cuff at company meetings, but never with any detail, and always spoken, not in writing. The numbers were thrown out like breadcrumbs for employees to consume, then move on. So it felt satisfying to see details here presented big and bold on the screen. But she tried to reconcile the numbers she was seeing with what she'd heard—at meetings and the previous day.

"Are the revenue numbers *actual*...?" Jillian guessed Desmond was repeating back the question as if a little insulted by it to stall for time. "Of course!" He nodded, reaffirming the $500,000 figure on the screen. He clicked to the next slide and began talking about partners.

Ian stopped him mid-sentence. "Can you break down for me where that revenue is coming from? I'm looking at the number of hotels in your pilot, and the number of events held, and I'm not seeing the $500,000."

Jillian knew Desmond would be feeling edgy now, but only a little bit. He had shown before he could wiggle out of any situation, head held high.

"Of course. It's all recurring revenue. To give a realistic scope of the success with partners, I've calculated revenue on the fees they'll be paying once the pilots convert into contracts."

"Recurring revenue is good. But if you're basing on 100 percent conversion, that's flawed. How many companies do you have in the pilot?"

"Fifteen at the present time, but we have five more that are close to closing."

"Right. I can't count those. Rarely do 100 percent of pilots convert. Are any of those from the same flag, like Hyatt?"

"10."

"So 50 percent of your revenue is from one company, even if it's the mothership. That puts your revenue number, even if projected and not actual, in a very vulnerable position. What if there's a policy or budgeting change in any of those companies? Wouldn't this be one of the first expenses to go? Corporate social responsibility is a 'nice to have' expense, not essential."

Jillian spoke up, feeling a responsibility to defend her part of the company. "My segment of the business is the hotel participation. Corporate social responsibility is actually a huge marketing play for hotels. As is loyalty program marketing. So when they can offer new opportunities to guests, especially business travelers, they get really excited. This is a big growth opportunity for them and a competitive edge. I think you can expect the hotel revenue to really take off in the next six months as these partnerships go into contract."

Ian thought this over. "Wouldn't it be true," he finally said, "that even if you grow hotel participation, it's meaningless if you don't grow traveler and nonprofit participation at the same rate? I mean, who cares if you have 100,000 new hotels, if you don't have any new events held? The hotels will see no ROI, so withdraw."

This was something she had personally been concerned about and had voiced several times to Desmond, who always dismissed it.

"You are absolutely right, Ian," Desmond said. Jillian had seen him use this strategy before in debate: agree with the skeptic, gently arguing the point while appearing to agree. "I'm in final talks with a new hire to handle nonprofit partnerships, with the subject matter expertise parallel to what Jillian has in hospitality."

Jillian turned her face to the wall of glass along the far side of the room, not wanting to give away her thoughts. A new hire was news to her. Through the glass door she could see two women in cut-up denim and black T-shirts walking down the hall, heads together and laughing.

Ian's eyebrows knit. "Actually, the conversation brings me to my next question. How do your expenses play into this? Added head count will be expensive."

"Of course. You're right. But just like in Jillian's case, while the salary expense will be consistent each month, the resulting revenue will grow exponentially."

"Okay, makes sense," Ian said, still not looking at Desmond. Jillian was glad she had taken the seat at the far end of the table where she could observe the dynamic between the two of them. Desmond moved to the next slides and finished his pitch.

"So what are the next steps?" Desmond asked. It was his go-to closing line, which Jillian always thought a little weak. The sales professional in her knew to ask for the sale—in this case, the money.

"Honestly, there are a couple things I like about what you're doing. But I don't want to waste your time. I'm not going to give you the standard, 'I'll talk to the partners and get back to you.'"

Desmond's smile loosened, like a child who just realized he would not be getting away with his mischief.

"I have some serious questions about the viability of the company. The numbers don't add up. It feels like an optimistic enterprise, and I can't build my investment portfolio on optimism. Or at least any optimism needs a rock-solid foundation."

He stood up from the table, and they followed suit. "So I wish you luck, and as a point of honest feedback, would urge you to get more concrete—and realistic—in the numbers you put in your deck."

That he said this so directly was a surprise. From what Jillian could tell, VCs rarely gave any feedback of value; they were generally cowards. Or maybe didn't consider founders worth the time it took to articulate their disdain. Or maybe they just didn't want to burn bridges. But this guy was blunt.

Jillian and Desmond walked through the parking lot to his car in silence. A breeze rattled the eucalyptus trees that lined the lot, wafting their faint medicinal scent. They were on Sand Hill Road, which was more than a street name. It was the Menlo Park mecca, epicenter of the VC world, where many of their offices were housed in low-slung '80s complexes. When you mentioned Sand Hill Road, everyone knew you were talking about capital. You could practically feel a charge in the air here, where millions of dollars were changing hands.

But not for Sojourner today. To deepen the wound, now they would need to weave through heavy traffic all the way up the peninsula to San Francisco and somehow find parking by the office.

At least the drive would be one-on-one time with Desmond, Jillian thought. Maybe they could have an honest conversation, forced to sit in the car. It was like trying to get a teenager to open up. The only time Christian let her into his high school life, was driving to and from school. "No eye contact, no escape," was her parenting mantra for these car conversations.

"What an asshole," Desmond said as he started the car. "And what a waste of time."

Jillian turned to him, then remembered the mantra and faced

forward again. They were snaking through a stately residential neighborhood, an enclave for Stanford professors. "You always complain that VCs don't give feedback. I thought he was very forthcoming and detailed. That's totally valuable."

"One man's opinion." Desmond's grip on the steering wheel tightened, as if he were willing the car to proceed.

"Well, feedback always is. But at least it's a data point. Any rational person would ask the questions he did."

"Investment doesn't come from rational probing. It comes from emotion. You need to capture the imagination of the VC. Get them to come along on the ride for the vision of what your company can be."

"I may be naive and old school, but doesn't the business need to make sense?" Jillian had now turned to look out the door window, not wanting Desmond to have any read on the tension that she felt in her face.

"Of course. But the VC has to have vision."

"Still, revenue and expenses need to add up, literally. Or at least be visible. These people all have MBAs and see hundreds of pitches a year. Yes, they want to be captivated. But they'd be foolish to not care whether the numbers make sense." This was so obvious to Jillian, and she was perplexed as to why Desmond could not see it.

"The holes Ian poked were worthless. Besides, I've been pitching a while. I've seen how it works."

That shut her down for a moment. Then she punched back: "Okay, that's probably true. And as you say, he's just one person. But you have nothing to lose by including a more detailed analysis of the financials in the deck. You have a gift for vision, so I'm sure you can do it better than most founders. In a totally compelling way, captivating their hearts *and* minds." She shrank back a little at her own ass-kissing but it was necessary.

Desmond kept his eyes on the road as he swung the car onto the freeway ramp, then shrugged. "Okay, maybe you're right. You may need to help me with that. You're good at seeing both sides."

She fingered the hem of her jacket and changed the subject to a partnership deal she was working on with a boutique hotel chain.

As she spoke, though, thoughts ran like a news ticker across the bottom of her mind. Doubts. He would never actually solicit her help. The next time she would see the deck would be in another investor meeting. Maybe figuring out with Trevor how they could get information from someone *besides* Desmond would be the best way to understand the company's financial status. Because clearly that information wasn't going to come from Desmond. Yes, it was a little underhanded. But it was for his own good—and the company's. They just wanted to help.

CHAPTER 15

When Scott suggested Jillian meet him for lunch a week later to get her out of the house during a work-from-home day, she jumped at the invitation. An hour later she had picked Scott up from On the Board, and they'd walked the two blocks to Nippon Sushi. Scott and Jillian frequented this hole-in-the-wall a few times a month, and the same two women always greeted them at the entrance—small, middle-aged and eager but speaking little English. The women recognized Scott and Jillian with shallow bows and broad smiles whenever they arrived, but did not know their names.

After they sat, Scott methodically unwrapped his chopsticks, and smoothed out the creases of the discarded paper, then rested the chopstick tips on his soy sauce bowl. This habit Jillian did not share.

She remembered her phone, tugged it from her purse, and saw a Slack notification. *Oh god.* She couldn't help but click through.

"What?" Scott glanced over at her phone.

"Maybe you can make sense of it. It's from Desmond." She read aloud: *Seriously short on cash and feeling backed into a corner. Just when we are making such headway. So wrong.*

Scott cocked his head. "What's the context? What's he referring to, and why is he telling you this?"

There *was* no context. Desmond often hurled angry or desperate thoughts onto Slack. If you responded logically, standing your ground, most often the response back was, "Sounds good." His original anger or desperation was nowhere to be seen. It typically left Jillian feeling angry and unsatisfied—that she had been needlessly provoked. Of course, none of the previous firebombs Jillian had received had been this serious, if what he said were true.

"This is totally out of the blue. At meetings, cash flow is never mentioned. And if I ask gently about it, he always says, 'No worries.' Now, this. How should I respond?"

"From a business owner's point of view, I'd say you should offer empathy and then any assistance. Not that he'll take it. You've tried pretty hard to help already, but he hasn't opened up."

"Sound advice." She pecked away at the phone screen, mostly one-handed, and showed Scott the message before hitting Send: *Oh no! How can I help or give support? I'll do whatever it takes for the company.*

Scott grimaced. "I'd delete the last sentence. Who knows what he could ask. Plus, it has a bit of a shallow ring to it."

"Right." And she deleted it and sent the message, then placing the phone face down on the table. "So, what sounds good to you?" she asked, moving right on as if the Sojourner crisis didn't exist. One of the small women was walking towards them, grinning, with her small order pad in hand.

After ordering, Jillian flipped the phone over, careful to still leave it on the table. Her notifications showed five Slack messages. Jillian threw a "can't help it" look at Scott and picked it up. Desmond had spewed a series of thoughts in Slack that didn't necessarily make sense, nor did they seem to add to a conversation about cash flow. She handed the phone to Scott for a look.

He raised his eyebrows. "Coming off the rails, I'd say. Why don't you call him up?"

"Oh, you're right. This is a serious conversation, not a thread quickly typed. Maybe I need more face-time in the office. Just when I'd settled into a remote routine that worked for me…."

"When you're in the office, does he talk to you? Or anyone else?"

She laughed. "Actually, no. So crazy—everyone sitting together, they just use Slack. So I guess it would have been no different if I were in the room. It's just that it would have been easier for me to tap him on the shoulder and say, 'Hey, let's take it outside.' Then duck into a conference room."

"You wouldn't have had me to suggest the face-to-face."

He was so endearing, and so right. Jillian smiled. Some may have taken his statement as arrogant, but Jillian knew better. Instead, Scott felt like her better angel. Like he was a part of her that rounded her out. Together, they were a whole. A team.

Now holding the phone in her hand, contemplating whether to call Desmond immediately and step outside the restaurant while she did, the phone vibrated.

Christian.

"Hey, sweetie," she said, making eye contact with a head nod to Scott. "To what do I owe this pleasure? I'm sitting here with your dad and we're having sushi."

"Well…give the Little Nippon ladies my best," Christian said. "I'll be quick but I thought you'd want to know about something I just heard. I had lunch with an old friend from college who works at Amber Capital. He told me about something crazy that went down at their company. With Desmond. My friend didn't know I have any connection to Sojourner. Anyway, apparently Desmond tried to strong-arm one of Amber Capital's partners into commitment to an investment. They knew each other in college, and I guess Desmond had dirt on the partner that he threatened to go public with. Sort of blackmail, founder-style."

"Oh my god! How serious was the dirt?"

"Well, I don't know what information Desmond had, if that's what you mean. But I do know the other Amber partners found out about it and were pissed—at Desmond. They immediately rejected the deal. Which actually called Desmond's bluff perfectly: if Desmond were to reveal whatever scandalous information he had, the VCs could turn it back on him. Desmond would never get a deal in the Valley again. Of course, word is getting around anyway, so...."

Jillian sunk in her chair like an exhausted child. The incident was disturbing. And terribly awkward: she couldn't let Desmond know she knew. Yet, what a condemning piece of information it was. At least without Desmond's side of the story. She wondered how it related to the message he sent earlier.

"Christian, what do you think I should do?"

"Well, I'm not sure there is anything to do. It doesn't really affect you. The plan got busted. Except that it's more evidence that you may not be working with the most upstanding CEO."

"Yeah, I got a disturbing message a couple hours ago, too. Any chance I could stop by your office later this afternoon? I could use your guidance."

Christian said he only had a few minutes but agreed to meet.

She put her phone away and met eyes with Scott. "You will not believe this." She thought for a second and then added, "Or maybe you will." And then she repeated the story.

"Crap. That's intense. Do you want to confront him on it?"

"No, he would just deny, deny, deny. Or spin it. So maybe Christian is right: just keep it in my back pocket as a data point. The other pieces of this that have come to light—that there's an undue burden on salary that seems out of line with our actual employees, and that our revenue numbers are misreported to investors—these things seem related but not really a through-line. I don't know if we can draw any actual conclusions from this."

Scott looked at her with empathy and reached across the table to envelop her wringing hands in his. "I'm afraid the only actual conclusion is that you should start looking for another job."

She sighed. "Harrumph. This one seemed so perfect. And I actually thought I could do something good for the world, too. Way to kill my buzz."

"Let's order an abundance of sushi and think happy thoughts until after lunch. That won't solve the situation, but it sure will help you feel better. Decide what to do on a satisfied stomach."

Once the last piece of sushi was gone, it became clear to her: whatever Desmond's predicament was, face-to-face was the only way to assess the situation. The straight-shooter in her lacked the patience to wait for things to unfold, so Scott dropped her at the BART station.

The elevator doors opened on the 12th floor, with its red neon *LET'S G3T S#!T DONE!* sign dominating the lobby. Ludicrous, really. It was almost an out-of-body experience to think that she was stepping into a WeWork office, with its hipster decor and free-flowing beer, to confront her CEO on whether he had been cooking the books. Oh god, she was so old-timey to even think that phrase, *cook the books.* It was like she had become a different person. She thought back to Westbrook, picturing herself sitting at her large walnut desk in her paneled, private office. What she had thought of as boring, now appealed as being safe. And beautifully sensible.

"I told you, you didn't need to come in, Jillian," Desmond said, looking up when she slid open the glass door to the office.

It was no big deal. She'd needed to come into the city for an appointment anyway. Or so she told him, a necessary lie. The others' eyes remained locked on their monitors, though Alex's screen blinked from Instagram into a colorful, cryptic screen of code. She didn't bother to sit down.

"I have less than an hour before my appointment, so why don't we catch up in the kitchen?" she said to Desmond. She knew the cafe-like area by the elevator would feel less threatening than a conference room. And while it wasn't totally private, no one who walked by would care enough to eavesdrop.

The hall was so narrow it was impossible to walk shoulder-to-shoulder. WeWork was brilliant at packing the maximum possible tenants per square foot, tenants so tickled by the startup hive ethos that they didn't notice. Or didn't care. By now, Jillian had become accustomed to walking the halls in staggered lines. Today it was a relief, as Desmond followed her.

They found an empty table and she sat opposite him. The chairs of turquoise painted metal were only comfortable enough for a short meeting or sack lunch. His hands were folded on the table.

She wanted to direct the conversation, to confine it to the general talk about cash flow, too nervous about how Desmond would react to her knowing he'd tried to blackmail a VC. Anyway, she didn't yet know how true it was. Maybe it was just a gossipy rumor. Well, that was the best-case scenario.

"So," she began, "the Slack message you sent was alarming."

Like a schoolboy, eyes on his hands and voice quiet, he acknowledged that he should stop using Slack so impulsively and apologized for undue concern.

Jillian resisted letting herself fall prey to his contrition. Her impulse was to say, "That's okay," to not let him feel bad. As forgiving as a child craving a parent's love. But it wasn't okay.

"Listen, you and everyone else should lighten up on Slack. If it's something important, have the discipline to say it out loud."

He nodded and she continued.

"But that's not the reason I wanted to talk to you. What you said about cash flow worries me. I don't think you've been transparent with me, or with anyone on the team, about our status."

As she could have predicted, he shuffled his feet, refolded his hands, and then put on a casual air. There was nothing to worry about.

"How can there be nothing to worry about?" she said. "From your Slack message, something's up. Only a couple weeks ago you sent me the financial reports, and from those it was obvious that our runway is really short, but at least there was a runway. Has something changed with the burn rate?"

He didn't say anything.

"I *know* you're worried about cash flow," she continued. "Don't you want some help—even if it's just a good listener—to figure it out?"

"Worried?"

"What was happening that caused you to panic? Can we make payroll for the next few months?"

"Months? I'm not sure."

For her, getting paid had always been an assumption of employment. Now at Sojourner, everything she assumed in business was turned upside down. She tried to reconcile what Christian said about blackmail, the Slack SOS, and the calm man sitting across from her. She then took a risk.

"So, Christian said he heard you were close to getting funding from Amber Capital, but that it fell through."

"Yeah, they're dicks." He shoved his phone in the pocket of his jeans and stood. "Sorry, but they are."

She sighed. She had hoped she would coax more from him. The conversation had gone as far as it was going. Jillian walked over to the elevator and punched the *down* button.

"My Hyatt appointment will close out the day. See you here tomorrow?"

He disappeared down the hall without turning to answer.

The appointment was actually with Christian. She walked the three blocks to his office, rushed by the rain and the agitation brought on by Desmond.

The lobby of Pier 45 Capital's office said "smart money," with sleek furniture and a polished receptionist who resembled Kylie Jenner. As the receptionist phoned Christian to let him know she was there, Jillian wondered what the girl did for the 50 minutes each hour when no one was in the lobby. Most likely her friendly veneer dissipated as she turned to her data analysis or whatever was on the monitor.

When Christian appeared, they hugged and he led her to his office. The room was small since he wasn't a partner, but it had all the trappings of the lobby, just lighter: framed prints that may or may not have been of value, a potted tree, and a blond wood desk without a single paper, just his MacBook Pro. Looking across the desk at the grown man, Jillian saw in Christian's face a flickering mosaic of moments from babyhood until now. But that was quickly wiped by the sobering reality.

"Sorry I only have a few minutes," he said. "What's up?"

She described Desmond's Slack message and the brief conversation she'd had with him. "First, a crazy Slack message. Then the story about blackmailing a VC. He's coming off the rails. And I'd like to know why. Or at least be able to help him. Any ideas on what I should do?"

"Yeah, I won't lie—that is concerning." Christian thought for a few seconds. "Do you have a relationship with your lead investor? If I remember right, it's Wanderer Ventures. They could be aware of the situation, so maybe you would learn something there. As long as you can have the conversation without making it look like you're going around Desmond's back."

Jillian shook her head, no. She'd heard Desmond speak to the partner, Rob Lockie, on the phone, but Desmond had orchestrated meetings so that the team would never meet the investor.

"Well, I think that's your next step," Christian said. "You're going to have to find a reason to introduce yourself and ask questions."

"I'm starting to think I should give up on this. Everything about it is outside my comfort zone, the sneaking around and all."

"Maybe your time would be better spent looking for another job," he said, sympathy in his voice as he stood to hug her goodbye.

"That's what your father said."

CHAPTER 16

After three decades in the event business, Jillian had built up a thick dislike of networking parties. So she had a definite resistance as she entered the half-ballroom at the Ritz-Carlton for the cocktail party benefiting the industry educational foundation and hosted by the local chapter of Meeting Planners International. She was there for the business opportunity and nothing more—an obligation, not a pleasure. Even if it was for a good cause.

Lavish greenery and whimsical touches of white and gold transformed the room. The crystal chandeliers cast a romantic softness over the room, despite being five o'clock in the afternoon and a room full of colleagues. Here and there, clusters of men and women in suits at high-top tables chatted as they ate. The suits (ties, even!) jarred her sensibilities, more used to seeing jeans and tee shirts at work lately. In the center, a long buffet table of hot and cold appetizers attracted a small crowd, as did the bar on the far wall. The vibe felt lively, even if she did not.

Jillian crossed the room, scanning for familiar faces. She had been to too many of these to be nervous, yet neither was she planning to enjoy herself. A small space opened at one end of the bar. She slipped in and ordered a glass of Sauvignon Blanc. Her back to the rest of the room, she watched the bartender's precise pour, appreciating his skill.

"Jillian!"

It usually happened this way. Someone she knew would suck her into the vortex. There would be shallow chatter, she'd finish the wine and be done with it.

She turned to see Shelley Harrison. This was luckier than Jillian had dared hope. Shelley had ten hotels under her wing as head of sales at the fastest growing brand of the decade, Bon Vivant, including the flagship property in San Francisco. Plus, until recently, she had been a powerful force at Hilton, which made her incredibly well connected. If Jillian could get Shelley's support for Sojourner, she'd have a serious influencer on board Sojourner. But so far, Jillian had not been able to get past Shelley's rigid gatekeeper, an executive assistant named Amanda. Until now.

Jillian gave Shelley a professional half-hug, then clinked her glass with a half-hearted smile. "To education."

"I heard you left Westbrook," Shelley said. "And I applaud what you did. Not many would have the guts to do that, to take a personal hit for others in the company. What are you up to now?"

"Living wage is a big issue for me, and companies pretend they care about it but they don't. That said, I'm in an easy position. *White privilege*, as they say. Anyway, I'm working at a startup now." She'd actually practiced her personal elevator speech in the mirror earlier in the day, based on advice from a coach on YouTube. She told Shelley about the mission of Sojourner, making a point to do it with honesty, not in a sales mode. Anyway, she truly believed they were offering something special, no sales hype needed. Shelley nodded. A positive sign.

"I've been calling you, Shelley—Amanda and I are practically best friends now—because my role is to align hotel partners with nonprofits for use of their empty meeting space. It's a win/win. You are able to utilize the room and for a good community cause. And just as importantly, you're offering a value-add to your most loyal guests."

"You said win/win. But there must be a downside. Is there a fee for venues to participate?"

"I won't hedge: there is. But most hotels treat it as a marketing expense. We've set up templates for how to market this as part of your loyalty program. So loyalty program members receive a personal invitation to an event when they check in. Plus you get to virtue-signal."

Shelley thought about this a moment, then asked about the nonprofits that would be participating. Jillian recited from the list of nonprofit partners, then described the event hosted by Mothers United for Veterans that she'd attended. Shelley was clearly interested, nodding.

"In a way, I envy you, Jillian. Don't get me wrong, I love my job. But I envy you doing something entirely new. Something untried."

Was Shelley's envy real or polite chatter? No matter. While she felt a little guilty about doing a sales pitch at a holiday party, Jillian had gotten this far.... She would ask for the sale.

"I just really believe in it. What do you think? Does Sojourner sound like something you can see Bon Vivant using?"

Shelley suggested a meeting, with a proposal in writing. "Tell Amanda I asked you to set it up."

Of course. Nothing of this scale could proceed on a handshake, though Jillian had secretly hoped she could lock down Shelley's support right then and there. But that would have been stupid. Impossible, she now realized. Still, this was progress.

A moment later they were joined by sales managers from two other hotels, and talk turned to gossip about industry promotions and firings. Jillian offered what she knew as if she were one of them, but she wondered if she weren't present if perhaps her own career change would have been a topic of conversation. She didn't have the energy to even think about pitching Sojourner to the others.

A discrete scan of the room yielded two other people she wanted to say hello to, hotel execs who were on her "target" list. Then she could leave in good conscience. She excused herself from the little circle and plotted her path through the room. With the two stops made quickly, just perfunctory greetings, a moment of small talk and, "You'll have to excuse me. I have an appointment, but it was so great to see you," she walked to the door.

Jillian felt lighter now, the wine warming her neck, and that glow rising to her face even as she placed her almost-empty glass on a table by the door. She should have eaten something. The band's bright rendition of *Yesterday* grew distant as she walked through the ballroom's foyer towards the escalator.

"Jillian? Sneaking out without saying hello?"

She turned to see Maria exiting the ladies room, hard to miss in a bright red poncho. Jillian resisted a comment on the outfit and hugged. "Actually, I didn't see you. Glad I caught you. My favorite MPI member," she said, grinning.

Maria wanted to know how things were going with Sojourner, and Jillian found herself willing to be candid. Certainly more candid than she would have been with the looser connections she'd spoken with in the ballroom.

"It's a totally different world, I have to say. A lot of fun. And it feels so good to be doing something I really care about."

Maria raised her eyebrows as if challenging Jillian to get to the real assessment.

"Well, yeah. It's not all rainbows and unicorns, of course. No place is. The CEO is a super nice guy, but I don't understand some of what's going on with the company, and he holds the cards very close to the vest. Especially for such a small team." Even though Maria was retired, she was still well connected in the hospitality scene, so Jillian felt it necessary to add, "But please keep that between you and me."

Maria nodded. "Of course. Are you by any chance playing the situation in a way that's too nice? I know that's your default mode.

But maybe if he seems like such a super nice guy, well, maybe he's not really. You could try to push him to the wall a bit. See if the facade comes down and you can learn what's really happening."

Jillian had never thought about her situation from this perspective. It made sense. If he was so nice, why did she end up feeling so bad when they partnered on things like investor meetings? Maria had the moxie to call Jillian on what was actually one of her most deceiving traits—a naturally nice disposition. It didn't always work to her benefit.

"Wow. You may be onto something, Maria. I'll need to noodle that. In the meantime, I'll let you get back to the party, but let's plan a lunch in a couple weeks. We're due."

They hugged again and Maria turned to the ballroom doors.

As Jillian stepped onto the escalator, she found herself smiling. This had been an hour well spent. Maria had touched a nerve that could really make a difference. Plus, she'd connected with a few colleagues in just the right way: conversations meaty enough to count, yet light enough to get her home in time to have dinner with Scott. He was the reward at the end of her daily discomfort, she thought as she reached the lobby. She jotted a quick text: *Pick me up at BART?*

It was funny. Since she joined Sojourner, BART had become her think tank, her chapel, the place she could consider the drama of the day and plan what to do next.

Working in sales much of her career, Jillian had always assumed she was an extrovert. But while she enjoyed colleagues, she needed time to think. She liked conversations that had structure, which is why sales meetings worked well for her. Afterwards she could process how the meeting went, then organize any follow-up conversations. Again, structured. And always requiring thinking.

Scott was a help with that, too, always a willing partner at processing the events of the day. She'd be curious to run Maria's conversation past him.

The next steps for Sojourner sales, though, were clear. She would call to set up an appointment with Shelley. Wouldn't Amanda be surprised? And send email notes to the last two fellows she chatted with, hoping for a meeting. Just as importantly, she would need to give some serious time to getting the sales deck into better shape.

Maybe it was the wine. Or maybe it was selling Sojourner at a social event for the first time. But hearing herself in the conversations tonight, she wondered what Shelley and the others really thought about Sojourner. Did they see serious holes? Perhaps she was just paranoid after Ian Sondquist's remarks, because on the face of it, her hotel colleagues seemed pretty intrigued.

Of course. They're intrigued because it's all solid.

Yet, as quickly as the thought came, she rebuffed it.

Too much like Desmond, that false confidence. Was it all solid?

She'd need to revisit that in the clarifying light of morning.

Her phone beeped with Scott's response. *Yeah, let's go get a drink. I need to talk to you about something.* Jillian let out a long sigh, unsure what that could mean.

CHAPTER 17

J illian didn't bring up the text until the bartender placed two glasses of Cabernet on cocktail napkins in front of them. It was a conversation done best seated at the bar, not across from each other, every facial expression noted. Scott didn't mince words.

"Jackson asked for a raise, a substantial raise, and I can't afford to give him one." He sighed.

Jillian knew what that meant without asking. Jackson was like a son to them and the business was to be his once Scott retired. They had agreed upon a plan that spanned ten years, with Jackson gradually drawing equity along with his salary. Although Jillian and Scott had never talked about it, they both knew he was underpaid.

Jillian put her hand on Scott's. "Oh god. That's a…, well, that's a pickle for sure. I mean, I know he deserves more and lord knows rents in the Bay Area are going crazy-high. I guess I always justified the situation with the fact that he had a future he was building in the business, with equity."

Scott's pursed his lips and nodded. "I already told him I'd swing it. I don't see any other choice. He's a great employee, and I can't afford to lose him." He glanced over at Jillian like he had done something wrong. "I'll figure it out. If things get really tight, we could maybe borrow from your parents. They've offered in the past…. But it feels totally messed up to take from the elderly. Especially with what they're going through with the dementia."

Jillian grimaced. "I'm the one who messed things up. I did such a noble thing, standing up for the hourly workers at Westbrook. And now look at us. I wish I'd never left. At least that job paid well and we could count on it."

Scott leaned over to Jillian and stroked her cheek. "Don't go there, Jillian. You're going do great things for Sojourner, and catapult it ahead. Things may be tight now, but I have no doubt you're going to be just what that company needs to get to Series A and fatter paychecks. And beyond!"

She let out a long sigh and then took a long swig of wine. If only.

A week later, Jillian was getting settled at her desk after her follow-up meeting with Shelley at the Bon Vivant, fumbling through her bag, looking for her notebook. She had left the meeting feeling buoyant. Confident. Optimistic even. Shelley had a few formalities she needed to complete before signing the contract, but they could easily be executed in the upcoming week.

"Holy shit." Trevor's outburst cut through the office and halted the keyboard clicks. Heads turned to him for an explanation.

"Did you see Desmond's Slack message? About payroll?" He had spun his chair around so he was facing everyone. "Holy shit," he repeated.

Now, without even seeing the Slack message, Jillian's enthusiasm flagged.

They were all in the office except Desmond. Which was not coincidental.

She tapped on her keyboard to read the message.

Friends: I am working through some cash flow issues, and unfortunately we will need to throttle back payroll for at least the next two pay periods. Across the board, we'll need to go to 60 percent of your gross pay, and this will be reflected in your paycheck beginning today. I know this is a hardship and am so appreciative of your loyalty as we build a system that will benefit thousands of nonprofits and their clients. In the meantime, as recognition of your goodwill, I will be increasing your equity, which ultimately may be even more valuable than cash. Again, I feel much gratitude for your work.

Jillian unconsciously had stopped her breath as she read. Sitting up straighter in her chair, she willed it back in rhythm and tried to relax her shoulders. It had been years since she and Scott had worried about money—probably when he first opened the store—but that anxiety returned immediately like muscle memory. So much for Scott's confidence in pulling her financial weight. Would they be able to get by? Her sudden stress was wrapped in anger at Desmond. He had posted this in the channel called #general, rather than messaging each person in the company individually. So wrong. Emotional intelligence 101.

"Well, at least we all know what's happening. Which is more than I can say for business as usual for this company," Trevor said with sarcasm.

Alex nodded and looked over at Jillian. "Have you heard any more details? He seems to confide in you."

She tried to put the thought of Scott out of her head and look relaxed. "I don't know about that. I'm in the dark as much as you guys." It wasn't 100 percent true, but in spirit it was. She realized it felt good to be on par with the group, rather than an outsider. Was this the ultimate—and saddest—way to be accepted by your peers: to be as clueless as everyone else about a pay cut?

Nate brought up what had become known as The Transparency Meeting, the all-hands when Desmond had presented the state of Sojourner financials. "There were no clues there that we were going to be facing this. How could things have changed so quickly? That meeting was just a couple weeks ago. Or were we just handed a bunch of lies at that meeting? Payroll doesn't lie."

Jillian felt compelled to defend Desmond. She wasn't sure why.

Did being the oldest person in the room mean you had to be the parent and stand up for the picked-on child? Even if that child was a CEO who made the decisions for the rest of them? Still, she couldn't resist the urge to defend.

"Let's not jump to conclusions without hearing what Desmond has to say," she said. "And maybe best not to attack him as a mob. I'm thinking, ask him privately. He'll most likely get defensive if everyone piles on, and if he's defensive the truth won't come out. The truth is the goal, right?" She had avoided saying the most obvious words: "He won't tell the truth."

She didn't know what to think herself. A week ago, the pay holdback wouldn't have mattered much to her personally. But now things were tight. Very tight. She also knew the rest of the team had little wiggle room when it came to necessities like paying the rent. Desmond lacked the courage to face them directly with the news.

She had a lot of questions, just like the rest of them. What was the plan for getting back to full paychecks? What about the promised equity bump? What were the details: how much and was there paperwork for this? She knew the answer, though, if she could admit it to herself. He had no intention of following through on it. Or, best-case scenario, his intentions were good but he lacked the focus to make it happen. There was no plan.

For the time being, she offered comfort to the others. She honestly felt sorry for them. And a little for herself.

The office cleared out before 5. Desmond never returned.

That night Jillian, holed up at home with her office door shut, ranted to Christian on Facetime. He listened patiently as she described the drama, though of course she couldn't let on that this had dire consequences for her and Scott. When she finished, Christian waited a silent five seconds, to be sure that was all she would spew.

"I won't sugar-coat it," he said. Inability to meet payroll, especially if unanticipated, was a major red flag. Not necessarily fatal, but it was what Christian called "a leading indicator."

Jillian did not want to hear this. "I've read all sorts of tales of founders who were nanoseconds away from having to close down, had maxed out credit cards and all that, yet were able to turn it around into a thriving business with an exit."

"Sure, that happens. But that's survivor bias. You don't hear about the actual failures at that precipice. Those founders do not write articles on Medium about it. The happy-ending-ers do. And I can guarantee, there are a lot more stories *not* written than otherwise. Sojourner now has a growing problem: Desmond is building up payroll debt. Yes, he can dig his way out if he gets funding. But he'll need to get it pretty quickly. Any news on that front?"

"Not a word."

"I'd make that my first priority: get a read on the funding opportunities. Keep in mind, it'll take a while for any deals to close. And I'd want to see proof from him, not his word. Ask to meet the lead investor or speak on the phone. I think you've learned you need documentation on everything, to trust him. Anyway, investors like to meet the team."

Jillian crossed her arms. She didn't like this shift from trust to wariness. She liked a workplace where she didn't need to worry about politics and could take everyone at their word. Somehow, she thought that in a very small company, there would be no games to play. Not so, apparently.

"Christian, what about the equity he offered?"

"Yeah, I'd definitely follow up on that if I were you. Everyone should have an amendment to their Stock Option Grant document that specifies what he's giving."

"So, what is that document? I know I should have a better handle on this, but it's all new to me."

After the kind of sigh that usually accompanied an eye roll when a teenager, Christian explained she received the Stock Option Grant—and signed it—with her employment agreement. "You should have a folder on your computer specifically for those documents so you can find them easily when you need to. And maybe a paper copy, too, knowing how you and Dad operate."

"It wasn't all that long ago that *everything* was paper. At least then you knew where to find things."

"I doubt it. How many days would it take to sift through that file cabinet you keep in the home office? I can do a digital search in seconds."

The sad truth, she realized right then, was that Christian now knew how to operate in the world better than she and Scott. Life hinged on an invisible see-saw fulcrum, and she and Scott were slowly descending towards incompetence as Christian ascended in competence.

Hastily, she ended the call. She was done. Done talking with Christian. Done with the digital age. Done with stock options paperwork. Done with Sojourner. Unfortunately, these were all things she actually could not walk away from.

Jillian sat at the desk for a few minutes, glad she hadn't had the conversation in the kitchen where Scott would have been listening. Sojourner felt so heavy right now. She missed the days when a manager would hand her a project, all mapped out, and she would just get to work on it. And finish it. In her worklife now, there was no finishing. Instead: keep pushing towards goals never reached, moving targets. In just two months at Sojourner, she'd already learned that the only way to stay sane was to not look too far ahead, nor too far behind.

She glanced around. Her home office was a million miles from the WeWork office, not 9. On the dark gray walls hung photos from their family travels, printed in black and white in antique silver frames. Christian on a surfboard. Scott in front of St. Peter's. Her parents in Bodega Bay. A bookcase housed years of reading, as well as a few plaques from MPI and Westbrook achievements. This room reflected decades and their milestones.

Scott appeared in the doorway, nubby old hoodie hanging from his shoulders. "Hey beautiful, you look lost."

The words were like a slap back to the present. Tomorrow she could dive in headlong. There was no use wasting a perfectly good evening with whatever mess Desmond had created.

"Let's take a walk."

"Now?"

"Yeah, I need some distraction, and the night air will do me good."

He pulled the hood over his head as she grabbed a jacket from the hook by the back door, and they stepped out into the very real world of craftsman cottages and an occasional stone apartment building, the air just starting to get heavy with fog.

CHAPTER 18

As she dressed for work, Jillian's Fitbit buzzed a split second before the notification popped up on her phone. The text was from Rob Lockie from Wanderer Ventures, Sojourner's lead investor. This was puzzling. After the conversation with Christian, she had been stumped about how to contact Lockie without going around Desmond so she had done nothing. Now, somehow, the problem had solved itself. The text asked if she could do a phone call at 9 "to catch up on what's happening on the ground with Sojourner." Absolutely.

That was in just 30 minutes, but at least it meant she would take the call at home, with the benefit of privacy. She jotted a quick message to Desmond to reschedule the meeting she'd put on his calendar to address the payroll issue, then pulled on a slouchy sweater and jeans, checking herself front and back in the mirror. She refilled her coffee cup and seated herself at the desk in her home office, waiting. She was almost physically itching with curiosity about what prompted this call. It was plausible that Lockie had 100 percent confidence in Desmond and he just wanted an update on her work.

That could be good news. Then why did she deep-down hope that Lockie suspected an impropriety with the books like she and Trevor did and could provide the transparency she and Trevor were searching for? Anger at Desmond, which she had been pushing down these months, was settling into her shadow self.

Minutes later, the phone rang, exactly as scheduled.

"Hi, Rob. Glad to meet you finally." Chipper, upbeat. This belied the fact that it was awkward starting a conversation with someone she'd never met, yet who basically controlled the finances of her company. And she had no idea where the conversation was headed.

"Me, too. Listen, Jillian, I really appreciate you taking my call. I wanted to have a candid conversation. I know you come to Sojourner with a ton of experience in hospitality, so I thought you might be a good person to talk with first."

She still did not know where this was going, but her mind caught on the word *candid*.

"I'm getting into the weeds with some expense line items for Sojourner," Lockie said. "I'm sure everything is absolutely fine, and I've discussed this with Desmond so we're not talking out of school, but I thought it might be helpful to speak to others to get a 360-degree view. In particular, I wanted to ask some questions about staffing."

"Okay, shoot."

"First, could you tell me the name of each person on the team and what their role is?"

This surprised Jillian—assuming he would have already known this—but she complied.

"Is there anyone besides you who would have an experience level greater than the others? Like, a senior developer or a VP-level person? I can see titles in LinkedIn, of course, but titles there are often not quite reflective of reality."

"Maybe Trevor? I'm not really sure, not knowing a lot of developers myself to compare."

Perhaps they'd established enough rapport that she could ask some questions of her own. She hesitated, not wanting to expose Desmond or seem disloyal, an instinct to protect him. But that's crazy. *Desmond* certainly wasn't putting employee interests first.

She took a breath. "You probably know that we've all been put on a pay holdback, right? Going forward we'll be paid 60 percent of our salaries."

There was a pause on the line. "No, I actually did not know that."

Guilt kicked in again. "Oh, maybe...," she stuttered.

"No, no, it's all right. All good. We're on the same team. I want nothing more than to have Sojourner thrive. Believe me, it's in my best interests as well as yours."

"Okay, thanks. Candidly, what do you think Sojourner's chances for survival are, if we can't make full payroll? I have to say, the crew is not too pleased about this."

"I can imagine. What did Desmond have to say?"

"Nothing really, except that we were in a short-term bind. He sent a group Slack message to announce this but he wasn't in the office to elaborate. And none of us have seen him since. I have a meeting lined up with him this morning."

"Shit. Sorry for the language, but...not the best communication strategy."

"Right."

"Well, I'll be straight-up with you. I know he's pitching for a new funding round but has not yet gotten any commitments. That's concerning. I've been trying to work with him on his pitch, which seems solid. But the red flag for me is that there are some extraordinary expenses in compensation on the balance sheet. Which he justifies, but I just don't see it."

A wave of relief, maybe validation, washed over her. She wasn't totally crazy if Lockie shared her same concerns. Presumably, based on even more information than she had. Now she was in the awkward position, though, caught between Desmond and his investor. She corrected herself silently, "*our* investor."

"So, does Desmond know about this call?"

His prolonged wait to answer, it seemed, *was* his answer. "No. But you should go ahead and mention it to him, I guess. Desmond should know that everyone does due diligence, including those on his same team."

Jillian ruminated as the BART train headed towards the city, descending into its tunnel under the bay, the sound now a roar against the cement tube's walls. Her emotions were jumbled. There was the uncertainty about Sojourner—its future and hers. That was oppressive. But it was mixed up with the sweetness of camaraderie with her teammates: she was not in this alone. And then the touch of flattery that Lockie had singled her out.

She had reserved a conference room for the rescheduled conversation with Desmond and went right there without stepping into the office. She didn't want to have to see the others. From the conference room, she Slacked Desmond to let him know she was there. It was a silent dance they did. And the dance, the physical moving around and the meaning it signaled, was like the unarticulated communication between partners.

He came in and sat without a smile or greeting. She imagined he knew why she'd set the meeting, so she didn't bother with small talk.

"There are a lot of questions around here from everyone. By everyone I mean, me, all the team, and even Rob Lockie." After she said it, it occurred to her that the others may have already spoken to Desmond, in which case this conversation would be repetitive. Just piling on.

Desmond looked at her, squinting. "You talked to Rob? He cocked his head slightly. Questions about what?"

"About what's going on with cash flow."

"Cash flow?"

"Payroll cut. Rob asking about salary levels. Seems like there's a major drain happening that's impacting cash flow."

This was not at all the kind of conversation she planned. His "I have no idea what you're talking about" face had provoked her. She hadn't meant to be accusatory but there was no turning back. So she continued.

"I'm going to start looking for another job. I love Sojourner, but I need to protect myself. And maybe it'll help Sojourner not to have my salary weighing the company down."

Desmond immediately threw himself into damage control, his face taut and straining. "We can't lose you, Jillian. Partnerships are essential to our success. And I'll have an impossible time convincing a fund to take us on if we don't have you on board."

"Please don't put this on me. You haven't had any luck so far, even *with* me. And while I've signed up hotel partners, they have no events to host—too few nonprofit partnerships. So I don't see that having me on the team has done any good. Except perhaps to give Trevor a confidant."

"Trevor confides in you? He's a developer for God's sake, not a high school girl. He doesn't need an office bestie."

She told him that Trevor had expressed concern about the financial state of the company.

Desmond shook his head, pushed back from the table but didn't get up, eyes on the floor. Jillian felt her own breath, in and out. She was sorry for him. But she resisted the pull to reassure.

He finally exited the room without another word, no goodbye. He left her alone with the cold truth: she would need a new job. She had said it as a threat, to scare him. But she could see it was true. Until this moment, there had been so much hope, even with the questions. It had been exciting, a thrill to join a company very different from Westbrook. One that was really trying to change the world. Now, the joke was on her. She was the stupid one for thinking this too-good-to-be-true opportunity would make her rich *and* save the world.

She checked notifications on her phone. There was an email from Shelley saying she completed the digital signatures for their partnership. Great, just great. Too little too late, it seemed.

Jillian sunk her head into her arms on the conference table. If only this could all go away. Unfortunately, she still had three meetings on the calendar for the day. Maybe it was better that way. Put one foot in front of the other, as her mother used to say.

The next day, Jillian slipped into her office chair and pulled it up to the desk at 9 a.m. sharp, a discipline that had served her well since she'd begun working remotely. She opened her email dutifully.

Jillian gasped as she read the first message in her inbox. From Maria.

Just saw this morning's edition of Avion. Congrats are in order for Sojourner and you: your CEO as Innovator of the Year? You're golden now!

Avion was a digital news outlet covering the travel industry, itself a startup less than five years old. In that time, though, Avion had become *the* must-read publication for everyone from airline executives to hotel marketers to travel agents.

"Whaaaaat?" Jillian said aloud, drawing it out. This was big. Totally surprising, but big. For a moment she tried to wrap her head around the contradictions here. On one hand, she was thrilled for the boost this could give the company. On the other hand, she knew that beneath the surface, his leadership was horrible and certainly not award-worthy.

She would put her hesitations aside. It was a huge vote of confidence from a respected publisher like Avion, which would reflect well on Sojourner and her ability to sell partnerships. Perhaps it would even bolster Desmond's ability to raise capital and keep them alive. How could the Innovator of the Year's company fail? That wasn't happening. Between this news and the signing of Bon Vivant, maybe they were turning a corner.

She sent an emoji-filled Slack message to the group, her way of celebrating with them long distance. They probably weren't even in the office yet, but she knew they monitored Slack religiously from home. Excited responses exploded back. Strangely, Desmond's was the most reserved of them all, though he was probably already a little numb: *Thanks. Only as good as the team.*

Jillian softened. That was sweet. She found herself thinking that maybe there was hope for Sojourner. And ultimately, that was a far better outcome than trying to find another job.

She typed a follow-up.

Hey, I don't want to sound too calculating, but what are the details in terms of when the award is given and publicizing it? I want to capitalize on the opportunity—my hotel contacts are going to be very impressed, and I want to jump on that sentiment to add a bunch of new partnerships.

Not sure, was his only response, with a shrug emoji.

That was puzzling. If it were her, she'd be nailing this down asap. It's for the good of the company, not an ego thing. Anyway, wouldn't Avion have communicated this already to him? Still, she didn't want to push him too hard. It was his award and his limelight.

There would be a gala in a few weeks, this she knew. She could totally picture the event, having attended several in the past. Desmond would be the star. Sure, some of the lessor innovators and their teams would be there, too—a few other companies were creating disruptive products in the travel space, also startups. They might even get honorable mention nods at the dinner, but yes, Desmond would be the star of the show.

The rest of the Sojourner team would be seated at a reserved table, everyone a little light-headed from the wine. Or maybe Champagne. The meal would be lovely, but the Sojourner table would hardly notice the food as they chatted about how far they'd come. As dessert was served, Avion's editor in chief would take the stage and introduce the award and explain why it was significant. Then he'd announce the winner, Desmond, lavishing praise. Desmond would approach the dais like an Oscar winner to receive the hardware, a bronze airplane mounted above a wood plaque. He'd give a lengthy acceptance speech, and Anna would be soaking it up when he attributed his success to her, making such intense eye contact with her that it would feel a little uncomfortable to the rest of the audience. But who could fault that?

Jillian smiled. She'd need a new dress.

Today, though, there was more practical action needed. She was itching to ride this award for all it was worth. She went online to see what she could learn and struck gold immediately: Avion just posted out a press release on PR Newswire that included the date, a mid-January affair. She copied the link and pasted it in the Slack channel, amidst the group chatter about the award.

Almost as an afterthought, she typed a quick private message to Trevor to share her renewed optimism: *Things are looking up, eh?* He responded immediately: *Maybe.* She shook that off. No one was going to bring her down. She was tired of feeling uncertain.

Fingers placed lightly on the keyboard, she thought for a moment and then got to work crafting the email to her prospect list.

CHAPTER 19

When Desmond wasn't turning up for the weekly all-hands meeting the following day, Jillian silently seethed. The rest of them made small talk around the conference room table while they waited, Trevor occasionally clicking his phone to check the time. Meanwhile, Jillian stared at the door. Finally Trevor grunted, "I guess he's not coming," and they all stood to return to the office, heads hung as if it were their defeat. Later she thought it regrettable that they had been too polite and let Desmond off the hook. At minimum, they could have sent him a "hey, where are you?" message. It was almost like they'd come to expect the no-show and felt they had no agency to require better.

"I guess the Innovator of the Year didn't have time for us," Trevor snarled as he walked down the hall.

For Jillian, the momentary sense of hope she'd felt the day before, bled out as quickly as it had come. Desmond crossed a line with that no-show, a line where Avion's accolades now seemed meaningless. Somehow today's behavior sent her tumbling farther than any of his past missteps. She felt done. Done with letting him off the hook.

Done with giving him the benefit of the doubt. Done with approaching the irregularities she'd seen at the company with optimism. Done with what she now felt was a naive trust. That had all just ended.

Jillian had several appointments at hotels on the calendar that afternoon. Somehow she would have preferred to stew in her anger. Yet she knew the meetings would fuel her in a more positive way. Sitting face-to-face with people she genuinely liked, convincing them to participate in a program to help nonprofits, having a goal to chase—the sale—and attaining it. This was the world where she had firm footing, a rootedness she desperately needed right now. She would not allow Desmond to contaminate these meetings.

Two hours later, elbowing her way through the Union Square crowds to keep pace, she ignored her phone buzzing in her tote. She was late for the Fairmont, with still one more hill to walk. And she'd need to allow a few moments in the lobby to get her breath, before being ready to sell.

When she reached the hotel, she paused under the black awning that led to the massive stone building. She smiled at the bellman as she turned away from him and pulled out the phone. It was a text.

Jillian, this is Anna. I'm having trouble reaching Desmond. Did he say anything about where he was going this afternoon? We had an appointment, and he didn't show up.

Anger rose again. Loops of complaints about Desmond ran through her mind. To not say where he was going, to not show up, it was habitual at Sojourner. But to do that to his wife? Really? She clicked through to look at Desmond's shared calendar. It was peculiar: there were no meetings, a totally clear day. Highly unusual. Even the all-hands meeting, which recurred weekly, was not there. He must have deleted it.

She ran through her mind for anything Desmond may have said, to piece together his whereabouts. Casual comments on meeting up with someone, or even about holing up by himself to work on something. Nothing. The day was as blank in her mind as it was on the screen.

Anna, he didn't say anything and his calendar is clear. I'm out of the office at a sales call but will Slack the rest of the team to see if they know anything. Will keep you posted.

She typed a message in the #general channel, so everyone would see it:

Anyone know what Desmond's up to this afternoon? Anna is trying to reach him. (Or Desmond, chime in if you're reading this.)

Jillian glanced at the time and would check back after the meeting. She took two deep breaths, the simple practice her yoga teacher taught for dealing with anxiety. Then she approached the front desk to let them know she had a meeting with Kathy Shields.

As she waited, she watched a man and woman step out of a large black SUV, the driver unloading two gigantic silver suitcases from the hatchback. The size of their bags gave them away as European, as did their fashion. Beautiful people. Young, but old money. She wondered what brought them to San Francisco. What would it feel like to be on a relaxed vacation in another country, rather than tangled in a morass of business stresses?

A voice came from behind: "Jillian!" Kathy was smiling, extending a hand. Reverie interrupted. Jillian relaxed. This was a world she controlled, where she could forget for 30 minutes about Desmond and his ability to throw all into turmoil without anyone knowing why.

The meeting went so well that Jillian forgot about Anna's text until she stood out in the daylight again. She checked her phone. Slack yielded no answers. A few responses included veiled anger that he skipped the all-hands meeting, but beyond that no one had a clue what Desmond was up to.

Thanks for checking in, everyone. I'll circle back with Anna. It's probably resolved now, anyway.

Now, to text the right thing to Anna. She thought for a moment.

Anna, I checked with the Sojourner crew and no one had any further information on Desmond's schedule. Hope all is well. Let me know when you track him down, so I won't worry.

Or should she instead say, *when you find him?* No, she preferred the more casual tone. She clicked to send.

Jillian continued on to her next appointment, at the Mark Hopkins on the other side of the square. These hulking stone hotels and the mansions of the Robber Barons presided over Nob Hill like kings of the mount, surveying the city below. Walking in their shadows lent a certain gravitas, an importance, to her mission.

Jillian would not allow herself to think about the concerns she had with Sojourner. Over the years, she had learned to stay focused. Thinking about challenges ahead was a sure-fire way to slow down. And she wanted to be totally on her game, focused and confident.

An hour later she left the Mark Hopkins feeling quite satisfied with herself. She had landed the deal. As soon as she stepped outside, though, that changed. She felt a vague sense of impending distress, like she had forgotten something on the stove. She shook it off. The bellman flagged her a taxi, and she watched the world go by as they made their way through traffic to the BART station. The indulgence of a cab—which she rarely allowed herself—was almost wasteful: the trip was all downhill.

As they texted during the train ride, Scott suggested dinner out to celebrate her successful sales calls. Nothing over-the-top, he said. Given her unsettled feeling—with the text from Anna and the earlier all-hands incident—it wasn't fully a day for celebrating, but she didn't want to cook either. So she agreed.

They walked to Le Mediterranee, their go-to neighborhood restaurant, a place Jillian likened to visiting a Greek island taverna: the food would never make the pages of a magazine but was wholly satisfying and always the cornerstone of a memorable evening.

The mahogany tables, Greek-blue napkins, and mismatched silverware brightened her mood somehow. Just a few other diners sat in the restaurant's dining room, with a few other tables occupied on the patio outside where they sat, tall space heaters enhancing what was an unusually pleasant early spring evening. "Such a weird day. Such a weird day," she repeated as they got settled. "I will tell you all about it. But first, wine."

After he made a simple toast, she took a sip of the wine and sat back. Even momentary thoughts of Desmond had a choking effect, like stretching a balloon neck and letting a screechy blurt of air out.

Scott let her sit in silence, until she was ready. Finally, she could speak. "Desmond is MIA. He didn't show for our all-hands meeting. Which was unprecedented, but not totally out of character. We were all pissed; I was *incredibly* pissed. He's totally undependable for meetings."

Scott nodded.

"But that's not all. I got a text from Anna that he didn't show up for some appointment they had. And she wanted to know if I knew where he was."

Scott cocked his head as her childhood Labrador had done. "Okay, that's odd. What do you think it means?"

"I have no idea. He has nothing, absolutely nothing, on his calendar for today. That never happens. Including the fact that the all-hands meeting would have been there because it's weekly for all of us. He would have had to manually delete it."

"Do you think there's any coincidence that you were probing him yesterday about the finances?"

"I can't imagine. I mean, I tried to be direct but I was never mean. And even if I were, how could that impact his schedule and cause him to disappear? Like would he fly to some VC appointment on the other side of the country and not tell anyone?"

"Good point," Scott said. They sipped their wine and pretended to survey the menu. When the server came to take their orders, it was a relief. Jillian ordered lamb kabobs, as did Scott. Always the same.

As the server turned to leave, they joked that they should be more interesting. "We really should break out of our pattern here, be more adventurous," she said. Scott agreed, but of course they both knew they would not change. The conversation diverted to safer topics for what was supposed to be an upbeat evening. They never came back to Sojourner.

After declining coffee and dessert, they strolled home hand in hand. In the last few years, the neighborhood had been overrun by millennials and college students, with their scooters, cropped tops and clunky black boots. To these youth, Scott and Jillian were no doubt ancient: *how sweet to hold hands at that age!* But in their own way Jillian and Scott were content as they walked, and Jillian thought about how lucky she was to be with someone who was still interesting after 30 years. Even thrilling, occasionally. As they turned onto their street, Scott offered to make tea and they could sit in the yard around the fire pit.

"That would be lovely," Jillian said, and then pulled out her phone without thinking as she walked to the back, remembering to flick the switch from silent mode. "Crap," she said out loud. There were numerous missed calls and a Slack direct message from Trevor, which she opened first.

Call me! Right away! PLEASE! No matter how late.

She clicked to call him.

Trevor didn't wait for her *hello*. "Oh my god, Jillian! It's about Desmond. He killed himself. Shot himself at their house in Tahoe."

Jillian gasped, unable to speak like the wind was knocked out of her in a fall. This was so far beyond what she'd imagined.

"I, uh, I don't know what to say," she managed to get out finally. "This is horrible. Poor Anna. Oh my god…. Are you OK, Trevor? I mean this is a lot to process."

"I guess. I have my brother here, and we're partway through a six-pack. I'll let you go, assuming Scott's there with you."

Jillian dropped into an Adirondack. She put the phone on the fire pit ledge and let her head fall back. The sky was filled with stars on such an unseasonably warm, moonless night, strangely quiet, disturbingly dark. It did not make sense, but it did. It couldn't be happening, but it was. Her mind was an arena of wrestling realities. She would need something stronger than tea to process this one.

CHAPTER 20

As Jillian watched the elevator's floor numbers tick by, her belly tightened. She'd seen enough death in her 54 years to know it had an unpredictable effect. It could bind people: she'd drawn so much closer to her mother when her grandmother died. And it could uncouple people, too: her best friend from college inexplicably refused to see her again when their mutual friend lost her battle with cancer. Grief took people out of character, exaggerating their every impulse. She figured that at Sojourner this could go either way: they would draw together as a team, rallying around the trauma, or they would disband, with every man for himself. She grimaced: right, all men but her.

In very concrete terms, there was the problem of their employment status. Putting aside the fact that someone they cared about had died, the fact was that they were all still employed by the company. There was a certain responsibility to Sojourner, Desmond or no. On the other hand, could the company even function now? Desmond held everything so tightly, secretly even. And there was absolutely no cross-training, or even collaboration, in the company.

Was there money for payroll, even at the 60 percent level that Desmond had enacted? Anyway, with Desmond gone, how could they raise any funds? Which meant despite the pay cut, they would surely be out of money very quickly.

Who would sort all this out? Jillian wondered as the doors to the 12th floor opened. The night before she had responded to Trevor's Slack message with expletives and emojis, and said she'd see him in the office in the morning. She couldn't deal with a phone call.

In the meantime, she'd sent a text to Anna with condolences. Beyond that, she didn't know what to say, so kept it short, to-the-point. One other thing she knew about death is that people overwhelmed with grief don't care what you say, they just care that you say *something*.

In her text, she omitted any mention of Sojourner. Anna would not be in any shape to deal with Jillian or Sojourner for a while anyway, so Jillian thought it best to give her some space. They could try to figure out how to proceed themselves, for now.

She wasn't sure everyone would show up, but as she turned the hallway corner she could see them beyond the glass wall. Just two empty seats, hers and Desmond's.

The others scarcely looked up as she entered the office. Chairs were pushed back from desks and turned inward, forming a loose circle. Alex and Trevor debated something loudly. Not exactly arguing, but there was definitely emotion around it.

She slipped in, attempting to fold into the circle without calling attention to herself. They were discussing something about the company's responsibility.

"What do you think, Jillian?" Alex asked.

"Sorry, the train was held up at the West Oakland stop. Back it up and give me a little context please."

Alex explained. They were unsure who would brief them on how Desmond's death would affect Sojourner or what would happen to their jobs.

"I was thinking about that, too," she said. "I mean, of course you guys probably already talked about this part of it, but I feel just awful about Desmond and the pain he must have been going through—whatever was the cause. And of course, Anna. But we can't do much about that now. So it's a valid question: what are we supposed to do, work-wise? And who has the authority to make decisions? Even, who has enough information to run the company?"

They were all nodding, first in respect for Desmond, then for their own self-interests and what would happen to their jobs.

"First off, I think we should talk to Rob Lockie, our investor. Does anyone have a decent relationship with him?" She looked around, purposely not immediately admitting her own conversation because she was curious whether he'd spoken to anyone else. No one moved or spoke. "Okay, I did speak to him once, so I can call him. He reached out to me with some questions, so at least I have that as a start."

Trevor stared at her. "Interesting. Why did he reach out?"

"Just to get a sense of whether the payroll expenses were in line with reality," she said, trying to sound casual, like it was meaningless. "He said he was going to be calling everyone, but it looks like he didn't get that far before this happened."

"Okay, well, I'm surprised you didn't mention that to me, since you and I been talking about payroll irregularities, too."

Trevor clearly considered himself snubbed. And the others nodded as if they were, too.

"Oh, please. Think about it. Should I have said, 'Hey everybody, the person who holds the purse strings to our company is not trusting the CEO's numbers. But shhhhh, don't tell Desmond. Would that have been productive?"

She couldn't read the faces. Maybe they said, *That's fair,* or just as likely*, You asshole.*

"Jillian, I nominate you to talk to Rob again," Alex said. "Learn more about how the company will function without Desmond. Until you get more information from him, I guess we continue with our work as if nothing has happened."

Nate, the quiet UX designer raised his hand and waited to be called on. Jillian looked down at her hands, so Trevor would play the leader and call on him. Which he did. "Do we know if there was a note?" Nate asked.

No one really knew.

"I'll go to a phone booth and see if I can reach Rob." Jillian paused a moment before standing. "God, I hope he already knows Desmond's dead, and I won't have to be the one to tell him."

Thankfully, the three phone booths at the end of the hall were all unoccupied. She selected the farthest one, then clicked off the phone booth's light switch and sat in the dark, the close quarters a strange comfort. She gave herself a few minutes of quiet, then ticked through a short mental list to cover with Rob. Note, payroll, acting leader. Note, payroll, acting leader. She had to treat it like a grocery list she didn't want to forget on a quick run to the store. The others were depending on her and they would ask about these things. She couldn't afford to forget even one.

"Jillian, I'm in total shock," Rob said without a hello upon picking up the call. Thank goodness he knew.

The conversation that followed flowed and halted like a sputtering car. They rambled, interrupted each other, and jumped the conversation around, the reality of Desmond being dead damping down thoughts mid-sentence. Finally, Jillian remembered her list.

"Rob, do you know if Desmond left a note?"

"No note, from what Anna said. That's a bitch, isn't it? Why leave us all wondering? Is it cruel or kind? I'm not sure. I'm guessing Desmond thought it was kind. But turns out that it has the opposite effect."

"Yeah, it gets you to start imagining things, conjuring stories. Which is never helpful. Listen, I hate to get all practical at a time like this, but the whole team is wondering…." She got that far but really couldn't say it.

"What it means for your jobs?"

Rob had a naturally calming way about him, and Jillian was relieved that he had anticipated the question.

By the time he finished telling Jillian that they did not need to worry for at least two pay periods, her shoulders softened.

"That's better for the team than I thought, honestly," she said finally. "But who is going to be making decisions, like whether to keep us at 60 percent payroll or go back to full pay? And who is going to decide the future of the company? Will there be a CEO or interim CEO?"

"That's the million-dollar question, isn't it," Rob said. "Desmond definitely had the controlling shares, and these would pass to Anna, which means she would have control of the company. And investors have some ownership, as well as any employees who have exercised options. I have left a message with the attorney for the company so that we can get confirmation on all this. There's no board yet, so I'd say in the meantime, Anna is running the company and making the decisions."

"That's crazy," Jillian said. "Not that she couldn't be capable. But she doesn't know anything about the day-to-day of the business. And it's not what we all signed up for."

"I'd be careful about what you allow yourself to think about her. For all you know, they had a confide-all type of marriage and she's totally up to speed on each and every issue the company is facing."

"Do you really think so?"

"Not necessarily. But it *could* be true. In the meantime, my own concern is protecting my investment. So I am hoping the entire team will step up and continue to work. At least until we have a sense of what's going to happen to the company."

"Right. Yeah. I agree. That shouldn't be a problem." Jillian was fixated on the idea that Anna would now own the company. She remembered thinking after the double-date dinner, "She's fun to hang out with for a couple hours, but I would not want to work for her." Oh boy.

Jillian and Rob wound down the conversation, and after hanging up, Jillian sat alone in the dark again. She hadn't had the guts to address what she most struggled with. But if she kept avoiding it, she'd never quell that sick feeling that plagued her. She picked up her phone and redialed Rob.

"There's something I wanted to ask you," she said when he picked up the phone, without offering a greeting.

"Hello to you, too, Jillian," he said.

"Do you think Desmond was engaging in any financial impropriety?"

Silence on the other end of the line. Impossible to interpret.

She continued. "Listen, I don't want to speak ill of the dead, which is why I wasn't brave enough to ask you a minute ago. We skirted around it when we first spoke last week. You had a lot of questions but you never said why you were asking. And I was too polite to press you on it. Now, everything's changed. Desmond couldn't have been feeling like Sojourner had a bright road ahead. Could he have painted himself—and Sojourner—into a corner?"

Rob drew a long breath, loud enough for Jillian to hear. "It's really hard to face questions like this when someone has died, isn't it? I've been struggling with that, too. The short answer is that I did suspect something was not quite right when we spoke last week. My fear is that Desmond was skimming money from the business. That said, I haven't found an actual money trail."

Jillian sighed, thanked him for being honest, and asked that he keep her informed. Now when she hung up, she felt worse.

She wanted to hide out in this phone booth in the dark, until it all went away. She did not want to walk back to the office and open the door on four people whose biggest question was whether they should keep coding.

CHAPTER 21

That afternoon as her homebound train emerged from under the Bay and the cell reception kicked back in, the text popped up. It had been a long day at the office as they all tried to work as if nothing was out of the ordinary, so when she saw a message from an unknown number, she sat up straighter and scrolled up to see message history. Anna.

I need to meet you tomorrow morning at the office to discuss some issues about Sojourner. Are you available at 10 a.m.? It's urgent.

A meeting on a Saturday? Jillian swore under her breath. She had hoped not to deal with Anna for a few more days. The funeral was scheduled for Wednesday, so she'd assumed Anna would have her hands full until then and wouldn't begin to deal with Sojourner until much later. Jillian swore again. What did this say about Anna that she was preoccupied with Sojourner when her husband had just died?

The next morning, Jillian waited at one of the 12th floor's kitchen tables, watching the elevator doors. She had given up trying to control her nervous tick, a jittery knee-knocking she'd done since childhood. Everything about this meeting felt off—the conflicted emotions behind death and business against a ghost-town backdrop of WeWork on a Saturday.

From what she could see, only one other person was on the 12th floor today, the Goth guy in the small office that housed a company called *Frumpy*. He was never *not* there, always hunched over his desk, usually in the dark, the oversized screen casting an eerie glow. Jillian wondered what kind of mission Frumpy had that required such intensity.

Finally, the elevator dinged at the same moment WeWork's "Your guest has arrived" notification on her phone did the same. Anna. The doors opened. Out stepped someone totally different from the person Jillian and Scott had dined with just weeks before. Anna's face was drawn, almost bony, and her pale skin dulled. She wore a black turtleneck, boyfriend jeans, and Doc Martin-style boots, more butch than her look that night at dinner certainly.

She stood and gave Anna a prolonged hug, aware of a vague sense that Anna's thin frame could be squeezed too tight and ribs broken. "Unbelievable," she uttered, finally, and let go.

Anna straightened. "Can we go into the office and talk? I assume no one else is here?"

"Certainly, we're alone. Everyone is just devastated, of course," she said as she led them down the hall, speaking over her shoulder as Anna followed. "We've just continued our work, not knowing what else to do." She flicked on the office light switch and the room came to life as if it were the start of a workday. She gestured for Anna to sit in Trevor's chair, and Jillian rolled her own chair closer and sat down.

"You said it was urgent. I can't imagine what you're going through. How can we help you?"

Anna, who had looked like a grieving widow moments ago, now pulled on a hard edge and her jaw tensed.

"Rob mentioned that he'd spoken with you, so you're probably aware that Desmond was the majority stockholder, so the stock now becomes mine."

Jillian understood the concept, based on what Rob told her, but she had no idea how that would play out in the day-to-day. But she didn't want to be rude by asking for details, thinking it wisest to change the subject. "He didn't have much in his workspace, but I boxed everything and I'm sure you'll want to take that with you."

Anna nodded, but she too answered with a non sequitur. "I thought I'd have an all-hands meeting next Friday. That'll allow me a couple days after the funeral to get my bearings. And I can get briefed on what each team member is working on. Get up-to-speed."

"Get up-to-speed for…?"

"For running the company."

Confusion and frustration rose immediately from her gut, and Jillian stuffed them back down her throat. She would hold her posture and her face expressionless. While inside she was a roiling mess of questions.

"Aren't shares somewhat irrelevant, given that the company has no assets, is not public, nor is ready for acquisition? So basically the shares have no value. Desmond was CEO because he had a vision for a company he founded, not because of his shares."

Anna didn't flinch. "Shares aren't irrelevant, according to my attorney. Anyway, you'll need leadership to continue."

"That is true. But how can you do that? I mean, that's tough to step into. A business where you don't know the day-to-day." It was direct but honest. At this point, there was no use for polite banter. Jillian's knees began knocking again.

Anna ignored the question. "The reason I wanted to meet with you today, the urgency, is so you could give me access to all Desmond's files. The accounting. The bank account."

What made her think Jillian would have access to these files?

"I have none of that," Jillian said, incredulous. "You can't run a company and give employees access to the funds. I know you know that, but it's such a crazy time for you. You'll need to go to the bank with a death certificate, marriage certificate, and all the documentation for them to give you access. Or at least that's what my mother had to do when my grandmother died. And I imagine there will be some extra layers of bureaucracy, since it's a business. Also, Desmond wasn't terribly transparent with the accounting here." The few documents Desmond had shared, she wasn't ready to hand over to Anna. At least not yet. Nor did she want to offer up Julie Strauss's name.

Anna let out a long sigh. Jillian's jaw clenched. She should really give Anna the benefit of the doubt, a widow trying to make sense of the affairs she was left with.

"Do you have any idea why he did it, Anna? I don't want to pry, but Rob told me there was no note."

Anna's eyes met Jillian's. That hard-edged resolve intensified. "Set up the all-hands meeting on Friday at 10 a.m., please, and add me to the calendar invites," she said. Anna handed Jillian her business card, presumably for the email address. "That'll get us started."

Jillian nodded. The fact that she had a week before the meeting to get a better handle on Sojourner's future provided a shallow measure of relief. If Anna would be taking the helm, Jillian wasn't sure she wanted any part of Sojourner, but at least she had time to think things through.

Neither woman spoke as they walked to the elevator. Under the circumstances, that felt quite natural. Jillian hugged Anna as the doors opened, hoping this simple act didn't bely her conflicted feelings. Once the elevator doors closed, she sank into one of the chairs in the kitchen. The meeting had lasted no more than 10 minutes, yet she was fully spent.

The emotions were complicated. She felt terrible sadness at what Desmond must have been feeling for it to end like this. And she was angry at having to deal with Anna, who was seemingly fraught with ulterior motives, yet Jillian wasn't sure what those were. And she felt guilty for feeling anything but grief at the fact that her boss had killed himself.

She sat up and took out her phone to text Rob, even though it was Saturday. Her phone rang back immediately.

"Thought it would be easier to have a conversation versus text," he said.

"Tell me again: is it true Anna can run the company now? And that she can manage the company's assets, including funds and payroll?" Jillian told him about her meeting.

"I believe it is true that she has inherited his shares, but it's unclear whether she becomes the CEO. It doesn't seem like a succession plan was set up—it would be rare at this early stage. But I don't believe Anna would provide the best leadership for the company. She has no CEO experience. Yes, she has a great sales record. But that doesn't necessarily apply to running a technology company."

"Well, she seems to believe that's what's going to happen. Which concerns me."

"What concerns me even more, as an investor in particular…." He paused as if wanting to retract what he hadn't even offered yet. Jillian leaned forward to reassure him of her trustworthiness. Then, with a sign, he continued. "Well, what concerns me is if she gains access to the funds. What I haven't told you is that right before Desmond died, I asked him about the unusual payments in payroll and to whom they were paid. He said they were for Anna, as the vice-chair and she was doing accounting work for Sojourner."

"That's crazy. I have never seen any evidence of her involvement. In fact, she didn't even know how to get access to his files, or to the bank accounts. She thought I could get her into the accounts."

Rob didn't answer right away. "I had hoped, maybe too optimistically, that this would all turn out to be a misunderstanding. But it's not looking that way. I'm going to speak with Desmond's attorney, well, Sojourner's attorney. Maybe he can shed some light on this. It's awkward as hell to be suspecting Anna of anything untoward when her husband just died. But I have a fiduciary duty to know what's going on and advise the other investors. That said, with the funeral coming up, I'll wait until at least Thursday to bring any of this to light."

"Maybe it'll be best if I do not schedule the meeting Anna requested for Friday," Jillian said. "I'll just act like I forgot. And I suspect any communication from you on Thursday could change the landscape, and that the all-hands meeting will be the least of her concerns."

"How's the rest of the team doing? And do you guys have a clear path for work in the meantime?"

The rest of them seemed to be doing better than she was, but perhaps that was a benefit of having a developer's mind, where life was a very clear combination of 0s and 1s. "Sure. We have had a pretty clear roadmap, so the work is no problem. And I suspect that we all find it a useful distraction. We'll be at the funeral, of course."

"Of course. My firm could hire a grief counselor for your team next week, if you think that could be helpful."

Jillian knew without giving it a second of thought that under these circumstances, a grief counselor would not be welcome.

"That's kind, Rob. I'll ask the team, but I think we're okay." She hoped that was true. She said good-bye to Rob and sat a few moments, taking it all in.

"Shoot," she said out loud. Anna had neglected to take Desmond's box of personal items.

CHAPTER 22

J illian and Scott stood in the church vestibule, the heavy doors closing behind them with a thud. Which echoed. Looking ahead down the long aisle of the nave, they could see only a handful of mourners. They were early. Traffic had been unusually light, like a favorable tailwind, and they'd made better time than expected. After sharing a resigned "let's do this" look, they walked up the aisle, slipping into an empty pew half-way up.

St. Mary of the Bay was nothing special as old churches went, yet it provided a gravitas Jillian was glad for. Sitting in the middle of the city's Financial District and out of place amidst the glass and steel of banks and brokerage houses that loomed above, St. Mary's had long since lost its residential parishioners and now served more for lunch hour Mass-goers and special events. Or so Jillian guessed.

Twelve-foot stained glass windows lined the walls, each depicting a Station of the Cross, and in the sanctuary a very plain stone altar was draped in black. A priest, not yet in his vestments, fussed at the tabernacle as an altar boy lit candles. The church was fragrant, with broad sprays of lilies on pedestals flanking the altar. Jillian knelt in the pew as a reflex, despite not having attended church in decades. She feigned prayer but let her mind wander and pondered the surreal nature of what was happening: Desmond's funeral. It was hard to grasp, really.

She stared at her folded hands, falsely pious, resting on the pew. The blond wood beneath was coated in a light grime, residue from hundreds of hands like hers, as parishioners gripped to stand and kneel, stand and kneel. Someone—no doubt a fidgety child—had scratched random lines into the dirt with a fingernail. *Sacred graffiti*, Jillian thought.

Eventually, the church began to fill up. As the other Sojourner employees came in one by one, Jillian would make eye contact, and they would slide in alongside. Jillian noted that none had brought a "plus one" except for herself.

Finally, Anna, dressed in a stylish black and white wrap dress, entered the church. She was surrounded by a small group of family, who guided her up the aisle and into her place in the front pew.

After a few minutes, Jillian glanced at her watch. With Anna seated, she wasn't sure what could be the holdup. She turned to the back of the church. In the darkened vestibule, one could barely make out the purple robes of the priest, but not his face. High above, in the choir loft, the organist played Bach with uninspired diligence. Even from the back, his cheap suit looked out of place. Hired help.

Finally, the organist transitioned to "Come Holy Ghost," and the congregation stood as the priest began his walk down the center aisle to the altar. He was preceded by the altar boy and girl, oversized candles held high, almost cherubic in their long robes. The girl's Converse sneakers peeked from beneath with each step.

The hymn brought back so many memories, the remains of 18 years spent under her parents' roof. They were traditional Catholics, but from a young age Jillian had some serious questions about the Church and religion in general, so once she went to college she asserted her spiritual independence. Today, Jillian declined to sing.

While Jillian held silent, Scott's voice was all-in. He no longer believed, but that didn't stop him from singing. It was Trevor's reverence, though, that surprised her. Not only did he sing in earnest, but only rarely did he glance at the hymnal for the words. She would have taken him for an atheist. But then, Desmond showed no signs of being religious and here they were. She'd always thought a belief in the afterlife was merely the human delusion that we are important enough to live forever. Well, she supposed it was a delusion worth indulging at a time like this.

The priest placed the bible on the altar, while the children stood the candles safely in their stands and moved to chairs at the side. Turning to face the congregation, arms raised, the priest began. "We're gathered this morning to celebrate the life of Desmond Hensley."

Jillian grimaced. This did not feel like a celebration. She chided herself and looked down at the half-sheet program in her hand to see what was next. She should give the respect due to the dead.

A luncheon was held after the Mass at Desmond's club. Jillian had once overheard him mention The Peabody to someone on the phone. At first, she had been surprised he would splurge on this luxury. However, The Peabody had a reputation for attracting a young, entrepreneurial membership, with the amenities to do it—killer fitness classes, a whisky-focused bar, and events like "Defeating Your Archnemesis" that appealed to the well heeled startup crowd. It was a running joke in her hospitality circles that these young CEOs needed someplace to gather when Burning Man was not taking place. So really, she rationalized (and maybe Desmond did, too), The Peabody was in keeping with what it meant to be a founder in San Francisco these days. Maybe, too, it put Desmond in a social circle with the VIP tech crowd in the city, a strategic move.

The club was within walking distance of the church. Once the priest and Anna filed down the aisle and outside, the rest of the mourners followed, chatting a little in the small plaza in front of the church, then slowly migrating in clusters up the sidewalk. When

Jillian and Scott reached The Peabody and she looked up at the facade, Jillian was reluctantly impressed. The Beaux Art architecture stood out on an otherwise bland block, wedged between two high rises circa 1980. You had a sense the stone and columned edifice was reserved for retired supreme court justices and banker-barons.

But once they stepped out of the sun and into the club vestibule, it was clear that this was not a place for those who valued precedent. The decor was edgy, with the lobby dominated by a life-size wood-carved giraffe. To the side, wingback chairs that were upholstered in a disco-y metallic fabric were arranged in a circle. Over a stone fireplace, a framed painting was a patchwork of acrylic swaths in variations of black. Jillian and Scott raised eyebrows at each other and followed the stream of funeral-goers into a large private room at the end of a hall.

There was no avoiding Anna here. She stood near the door, as if in a wedding's receiving line. How did Anna even get to the club before they did? No matter, they would wait in line. When they finally reached Anna, Jillian hugged her, offering a few words this time, though later she couldn't remember what they had been. The rest of the Sojourner team had also somehow arrived before Jillian and Scott, and they were huddled in one corner, trying to appear like they belonged. There was a protocol to these things Jillian knew: one must straddle the line between being pleasantly social and showing respect for the grief in the room. Jillian and Scott joined the small circle, and she made an effort at small talk, feeling a responsibility to put all at ease. Then Scott jumped in and did a better job at this, or perhaps it was just more genuine.

As he did, she scanned the room. Rob Lockie stood at the center of a cluster of smartly dressed millennials. She'd never met him in person, but she could make out the voice like a faint radar ping. The others from Sojourner would not recognize him. She kept watch.

Before long, a procession of men in white jackets carried silver chafing dishes to the skirted table along the far wall. Lunch was served. The room's mood brightened and the chatter level rose, as groups moved towards the food. Then, full plates in hand, people found seating at tables scattered throughout the dark-paneled room, with new acquaintances introducing themselves as they sat down. "How did you know Desmond?" they would say.

After eating, Jillian and Scott excused themselves from the Sojourner group, and she grabbed Scott's hand to lead him to the far side of the room. She had spotted Rob eating at a high top, momentarily alone.

"Rob, tragic, isn't it?" Jillian said. Rob nodded.

Scott reached out his hand, knowing exactly who he was going to be introduced to. "I'm Scott Johnson, Jillian's husband. Obviously." He gestured to Jillian at his side, not realizing Rob and Jillian hadn't met in person. "I very much appreciate how candid you've been with Jillian about what's happening at Sojourner."

Leave it to Scott to break the ice, Jillian thought. His unaffected naivete was one of the reasons she fell in love with him, and it served them both well in this moment. She would not have had the nerve to bring up what was going on at Sojourner so quickly. Rob's face opened up like a moment of sunshine on a cloudy day as he shook Scott's hand.

Rob turned to Jillian and nodded more solemnly in greeting. "This is all so hard, but the reality is there's a business to tend to. I've learned some things since we spoke, but we shouldn't deal with them today. I'll call you tomorrow. We can figure out together how to talk to Anna—I think I've deciphered her game. But I'll call you."

Jillian nodded, and Rob picked up his plate, placed his utensils across it, and walked away. She turned to Scott.

"Isn't that just fucking great?" Scott would understand. She was just so tired of the drama.

"You deserve a glass of wine. It's an occasion that deserves day drinking, and I'm driving."

He did understand. She had no inclination to stop him, as he turned to the bar and brought her a glass of Chardonnay.

"My tried-and-true hotel world is seeming quite appealing now," she said, taking a sip. "Yes, they paid unfairly. Yes, it was a bit too predictable. But this is more adventure and grief—literally—than I bargained for. And I'm not sure it's exactly highly principled."

"Cheers," Scott said wryly. He raised an invisible glass to hers, as they watched Anna at the far side of the room, like a celebrity in the center of a circle of mourners. There was something about that which seemed fitting. She did not shun the attention, that Anna. Scott and Jillian gave each other a knowing look, no words necessary.

CHAPTER 23

T he mood at the office the next day was subdued. Jillian had not wanted to get out of bed, and she imagined the rest felt the same. She didn't feel like talking, and she didn't feel like working. Yes, her body occupied a space at the desk, but she scrolled aimlessly through files. The others had work screens up and headphones on, but there wasn't much keyboard clicking. They too were languishing.

When a text lit up her phone without a contact name, Jillian assumed it was from Anna.

Could you please schedule an all-hands meeting for tomorrow at 10? Attendance mandatory. There are a number of things I'd like to discuss with the full group.

Oh. It was actually not from Anna but from Rob Lockie. She slumped. Could he be announcing that the company would shut down?

Puzzled, she recalled Anna had also requested a meeting Friday, which Jillian purposely neglected to schedule. Anna had not followed up. Perhaps Rob's meeting was actually Anna's? Jillian thought carefully about how to respond, then typed:

Of course. But Anna asked for a meeting tomorrow as well. You suggested I not schedule it, so I haven't. Have you spoken with her? Are you positive she's not expecting a meeting?

The answer came immediately.

No. I've already had several calls with Anna and she no longer will be meeting with you. I'll fill you in when we're together.

Jillian's grip on the phone softened. She trusted Rob in a way she didn't trust Anna, even if he brought bad news.

She cleared her throat, then slid her chair back from the desk to signal that what she was about to say was important. She cleared her throat again. "So guys, just so you know...."

In light of the uncertain mood at Sojourner, she thought it best to have a short conversation about the meeting rather than just send out a calendar invite with no explanation, Desmond-style.

They removed their hands from the keyboards almost as if choreographed and swung around to face her. In this room, that was the highest form of respect. At so many meetings, Jillian had bristled when others were scrolling on their phones or typing, heads down, while someone addressed the group. In the business world she grew up in, people actually jotted notes on yellow pads during meetings because they wanted to remember what was said. In the old days, the worst breach of meeting etiquette was whispering to a coworker. Now the whisper was digital—sometimes her coworkers used Slack as a back channel to make comments on someone speaking at a meeting. Yes, attention was rarely given these days, but at this moment it was.

"Rob Lockie wants to have a meeting with all of us tomorrow at 10. I have no idea what it's about, but he said he wants to fill us in on some developments."

"Do you think he's shutting us down?" Alex asked, voicing what was on all their minds.

"That's my fear, but he didn't say, and I really have no idea. When we spoke after Desmond died, he said we're all good for a while. At least two pay periods. At the luncheon yesterday, though, he said he had new information from Anna. So let's be optimistic. Maybe he wants a meeting to reassure us? Like a coach giving a pep talk?"

The others looked at her as if taking issue with this in collective silence.

"Listen," she said finally, "I know we're in a tough spot, but we have to have compassion for what Desmond was going through. And I have absolutely no idea what Rob has to say. Or what kind of provisions Desmond may or may not have made. I know it's hard and we're all upset, but let's just wait until tomorrow before making judgments. Let's keep our heads down, do the work, and then deal with whatever the meeting brings. I'll send a calendar invite to everyone."

Heads barely nodding, they turned back to their screens.

Jillian reserved the large conference room for the meeting, and she met Rob at the elevators when he arrived, offering a cup of coffee from the adjacent kitchen before heading to the room together. The rest of the team had already gathered, most with their phones in front of them on the table, not bothering to bring a laptop as they would to a working meeting. This was not a meeting for notes.

"Everyone's a little wound up," she said to Rob as they walked. "They don't know what the message is, but I've warned them not to shoot the messenger."

"Not sure I like the picture that conjures." Neither smiled at the joke.

As Jillian pulled open the conference room's glass slider door, her warning was confirmed. The tension hit them like a blast of below-zero air.

She tried to smile. "If you didn't meet him at the funeral, this is Rob. Rob, this is everyone." She gestured to an empty chair for him, and for a moment she felt sorry for herself. Why was *she* the one orchestrating this? She didn't appreciate the role of Team Mom.

Rob took his seat and made a few light comments about the building and traffic. The group warmed a little. He asked them to introduce themselves, and answered with a kind comment to each introduction, based on what Desmond had told him about the team.

"Okay, so I'm glad to meet you all, though we can all agree that the circumstances suck. But I want to be straight with you. You've probably been wondering since Desmond died: what does this mean for Sojourner?

"First, the crappy news that informs all the rest of the conversation. We've learned this week that Desmond was involved with some under-the-table and probably fraudulent actions. And Anna may have been involved as well. Which is why I would respectfully ask that you not have any conversations with her."

Jillian stopped breathing, this news putting a chokehold on her. A barrage of curses went around the table. Even with the suspicions she and Trevor had, this was a blow. The reality of the word *fraudulent*, spoken plainly under the fluorescent lights of a conference room made the truth too real. She had to make a conscious effort to let out that breath.

"Several other investors and I gained access to the financial records for the first time earlier this week. Desmond did not give us regular reports on cash, and when he did, we took him at his word. I know now this was a serious mistake, one I'll not be making again as an investor. The man had a certain charm that led us to trust him, I can see now in hindsight. The reality is that the liabilities of the company right now outweigh its assets. Once bills are paid, investors will receive a portion of their investment returned, and the company will have depleted all funds. As investors, we will all have lost much of our investment, and we will be attempting to redeem some of that. That said, we know you are as much victims in this as we are, so as I told Jillian previously, we will authorize paychecks for two further pay periods. Full pay, not 60 percent. I will be asking your help in tasks related to winding down the company, but I really don't expect work beyond that, so you don't necessarily need to show up to the office."

The silence around the table was heavy. The news was no surprise, but the finality, the clarity of it, was. It was painful to let go of Desmond's dreamy vision—innovation, changing the world, giving back, and maybe even an exit—which, as he always said, would make them all rich.

"Looking for a job sucks," Alex finally muttered under his breath.

"*Why* was Desmond doing this? And how does Anna play into it?" Jillian asked.

Rob explained that he had no knowledge of Desmond's motives but that an investigation had begun. Anna's role would be scrutinized and the couple's financial records would be combed through. "Sorry, but that's all I've got."

"What needs to happen to close down Sojourner?" Trevor asked, changing the subject.

"Honestly, this is all new territory for me," Rob said. "I am working closely with our attorney and the bank, and I have to assume they have experience with these processes. I promise that I will be totally upfront and open with you in the next weeks. Sojourner was a great concept and one I was proud to be associated with. I'm sad that Desmond took down the company with him. It looks like his depression was fueled by the temporary financial stress of the company, and maybe pressures within his marriage, and that he took all that on alone, not telling anyone who could actually help him."

"Sad," Jillian said—it was all she could manage—as she walked Rob to the elevator, leaving the rest to process their new reality around the table.

CHAPTER 24

As a rule, Jillian attacked uncertainty with activity. She knew that. Faced with Sojourner's demise, the twenty-somethings would get drunk. She would get things done.

At the office she created a master to-do list, a full page in her planner, a high-low mix of heavy tasks (Meet with attorney to void hotel partnerships) and light ones (Cancel Salesforce subscription). Still, while crossing off to-dos felt satisfying, it did not answer the looming questions.

What needed to happen legally to dissolve the company? What would happen to Anna? Were her actions criminal, or just distasteful to investors? Did her stake in the company give her free reign and protect her? Would the local startup community gossip about the improprieties? Would Sojourner be a black mark on each of their resumes?

A few days after Rob met with the team, Trevor rolled his chair back to sidle up to Jillian. "This is interesting," he said, a hanging introduction.

"What? Can't you see I'm super-busy positioning us for Series A?"

Jillian's sarcastic fake-irritation was easy to see through, and Trevor smiled.

"Hey, walk with me to the kitchen for a coffee refill." That meant Trevor had something to say without the others listening.

"I just got an email from Sarah James," he said as he filled his mug at the coffee urn. "I think she left Sojourner before you arrived."

"If I remember right, she was some kind of sales associate, that she'd set up appointments for Desmond to sell the program to nonprofits. Didn't you tell me she didn't like Desmond so left for another job?"

"That's right. I'll forward the email to you. But the upshot is that she heard about Desmond and wants to know about her shares."

"What does that mean?"

"Sarah exercised her stock options, leaving just after the one-year cliff. Now she's wondering about the shares' value."

Jillian sighed. Stock options was a subject so complex that it usually shut her brain down. And it seemed irrelevant at this point in Sojourner's life. "If the company is going under, they're not worth anything, are they?" she asked.

"Right, Sherlock. They never actually were worth anything until she could sell them. Which means the company would have had to have an exit—Sojourner would need to be acquired or go public."

"IPO? I don't see that could ever have happened. Acquisition, maybe. Eventually. Though we were a long way from being attractive enough for that."

"Right. It always irked me that Desmond talked about equity like it was a big deal, like he was being so magnanimous in giving it to us. But we were nowhere near being in a position where equity could have value."

Jillian thought about how she'd glossed over her employment documentation and hadn't really understood the stock options paperwork. Her cousin was an attorney and she'd sent the paperwork to him for a quick review, which he just replied to by saying, "Looks boilerplate, didn't see any issues. Congratulations!" Christian had concurred.

"Dumb question, but what's the cliff?"

Trevor explained that you had to work at Sojourner for one year before you could exercise any options or actually buy stock. It was incentive to stick around for at least a year, and was standard practice.

"I was too smart about options for my own good, as it turns out." Trevor explained that he made it a practice to buy shares as they vested. By exercising earlier—most people exercised when they left the company—he locked in a lower share price. "Mistake, it turns out," he said. "Granted, my strike price was low, but obviously, they turned out to be worth nothing. So I basically paid in advance for something that lost all value."

"Ouch." The fact that she never even made it to the cliff somehow felt like a loss, a future robbed from her by Desmond.

Trevor shrugged. "Maybe Sarah and I got lucky, though, and in liquidation there will be money left over after the investors, who have preferred shares, get their due. I doubt it, but I'm sending Sarah to Rob to figure it out. Stock. That's the least of my concerns."

Jillian knew Trevor was looking for a new job. None of them were hiding the fact that this took precedence over any work wrapping things up at Sojourner, and she got that. But somehow she couldn't get into that mode herself. She felt herself clinging to Sojourner.

"How's the job hunt going? You should have no trouble finding something. Developers are in high demand, right?"

"After this experience, I'm trying to be choosy. No more early stage. I'm looking at Series B and beyond."

"Meaning?"

"Meaning companies that are really solid in their funding, are less up and down, and with tons of perks."

"Really? A ping pong table is a lure for you? You have free beer here."

He laughed. She was finally getting comfortable with using sarcasm with him. Then he said, "Did you know that at companies where lunch is provided, that's a value of more than $10,000 a year in compensation?" He seemed serious.

"I'm no math genius, but that sounds high."

Trevor looked embarrassed. "Yeah, well, maybe so. My buddy gave me that stat when he was looking for a job. But you get the general idea."

Jillian sometimes felt like she had landed on a different planet. She still packed a lunch for herself on days she went into the office, scavenging her refrigerator for leftovers to scoop into Tupperware. She tried to picture herself at a job that provided lunch, napping pods, and beer pong tournaments. Somehow, it felt too ridiculous.

"I have no doubt you'll land on your feet, Trevor," she said.

"The thing is, I really believed in what we're doing here. It sucks that it died with Desmond."

She thought about how far the company had come and what a waste it was that it went off its own cliff.

"You know, we were on a pretty solid path," she said. "And the problem right now is cash. So crazy idea: do you think it would be possible to reorganize? Isn't that what bankruptcy is all about? And maybe *we* could get funding to run the company—the right way this time."

Trevor didn't answer, but his face showed he was thinking ahead, chewing on it, curious even.

She continued. "There's no harm in asking Rob about it. He bought into the company once, he may be willing to do it again, if he had total confidence in the cast of characters—us."

"And full financial transparency."

"Exactly."

They agreed to think about it over the weekend, and if it still seemed like a viable idea the following week, they would set up a meeting with Rob.

Jillian decided to stop by On the Board on her way home. As she walked down Ashby Street she marveled. The low sun cast pink shadows on funky storefronts and the mashup of college students and aging hippies buoyed her. How lucky they were to have the shop so close to their home. She'd gotten used to this, but Scott was the kind of person who never took this for granted, the poster child for the gratitude movement. His indefatigable disposition had saved her from herself many times over.

The old-fashioned bell tinkled as she pulled open the door. Murals of snowscapes and skateboard parks signaled a different world upon entering On the Board. If you were under 30 and slightly rebellious, you were coming home here. For the rest of the universe, you were just a tourist in a funky board shop. The store was empty except for Scott and Jackson. Scott was grooming Jackson to take over the business when he retired. The kid was a 25-year-old snow bum with an entrepreneurial streak and a hard-working nature.

"Hi, guys," Jillian said lightly. Scott's immediate puppy-at-the-front-door, tail-wagging look made the side trip totally worthwhile. She gave him a big hug, and followed up by embracing Jackson a little more lightly.

"I see you're raking in the bucks here today," she added, with a nod to the empty aisles. So much sarcasm lately.

"Actually, it was a very solid day," Scott said, winking at Jackson. Scott told Jillian they had just sold a family of four full snowboard gear, including a couple jackets for the kids. "How about for you? Or dare I ask?"

"Well, considering that I'm currently working for a company that is on its last breath, I'm not exactly on an upward curve. But something interesting came up today that I'm dying to hear what you think of."

Jackson shuffled towards the back room. "Sounds personal. Maybe I'll call it a day."

"No wait, Jackson. I'd love your thoughts, too."

He returned to Scott's side, hands in his jeans pockets.

"So…." She took a deep breath, then spoke in detail about her idea to relaunch Sojourner. "Do you think it's even worth talking about? That we could resurrect the company without Desmond?"

The men looked at each other. "Just to play devil's advocate…," Jackson said tentatively, "but wouldn't the investors have already thought of this? I mean, if it were possible?"

"Good point, but I don't want to make that assumption. Maybe they couldn't see the forest for the trees, being so close to having to unravel the problems Desmond hid."

Scott nodded agreement and a big smile crossed his face. She knew it meant he was fully behind the idea. This was predictable but actually had the opposite effect: a cloud of skepticism moved in to cast a shadow on Jillian, negative thoughts swirling. What had she and Trevor been thinking? She really didn't have the skills to manage the company out of a bankruptcy. Leadership would naturally fall to her. The developers would be consumed with furthering the product. Which would leave the rest of it—management and the financial aspect of the company—to her. She'd never done this for a whole company before, just a department, albeit a large and profitable one.

Then for a second, she regained confidence. Could it really be rocket science?

That confidence dissipated quickly again, with a doubt that had been nagging at her. Jillian asked, "Do you think my age would be a negative for the company, if I were a, well, let's call it a re-founder?" Both men immediately shook their heads to the negative.

She wasn't satisfied. "Jackson…I'm looking at you. Think about people you know who are your age. Would they trust a company owner who looks like me? Board sports and startups—they're young persons' games."

He dug his hands deeper into his pockets. "I never think about your age. I never think about Scott's age. To me, it seems like we're the same age. I mean, logically, I know you guys are older than I am. But it really doesn't feel that way."

Jillian gave him an impulsive hug. He was so sweet, and she had the sense that what he said was honest. She didn't think of him as being younger either, except when they were literally talking about age. And the same was true of the team at Sojourner. Well, mostly.

"Okay, Scott, we can talk more about it at home. I'm just trying to get my head around the idea and want to have thought through any issues before Trevor and I talk about it with Rob. I don't want him to think we're totally crazy."

"No way!" Jackson said.

She gave him another hug.

"Let's close up a big five minutes early here, folks," Scott said. "We have a lot to talk about and there's no sense standing around here." He pulled his prized Cal keyring from the back pocket of his jeans, ready to lock up, and the three walked out into the early evening bustle of Ashby Avenue.

CHAPTER 25

Trevor put a meeting for Monday on her calendar titled, "Sojourner's Resurrection?" She appreciated the question mark.

Still, the timing gave her space to really consider the situation. After walking home from the shop Friday night, she and Scott talked over the resurrection possibilities while they cooked. Some of their most productive conversations happened while working through a recipe together, usually with wine involved. On this evening, they pulled together an herb-crusted pork tenderloin and mashed potatoes as they discussed whether making another go at Sojourner would be an opportunity or a debacle. When the digital thermometer reading had almost reached *done*, Jillian whipped the potatoes and Scott set the table. By the time they sat down to enjoy the meal, the conversation was getting intense.

Scott, despite his good-natured support, was good at playing devil's advocate. And as a business owner, he'd weathered plenty of obstacles: from employee theft to supplier bankruptcy. He argued for doing some serious financial analysis before committing: make the decision based on brain rather than heart. His only hesitation, he said, came from the fact that Jillian's love of the concept and desire to help nonprofits may keep her from seeing some realities. *Once fooled, shame on you; twice fooled, shame on me,* he reminded her.

She countered. "So much more is clear now than it was when Desmond started the company." There was already traction. Wasn't the fact that she had easily put together hotel partnerships proof of concept? Plus, without Desmond draining the coffers they had a clear shot at profitability—especially with someone like Rob Lockie advising them.

Scott admitted defeat and clinked her wine glass. "To profitability. Plus passion." The better-days-ahead optimism had returned. *I've got this*, she thought, the first time she'd applied the phrase to herself. It was an indulgence, she knew, but she wanted Sojourner to work.

In the back of her head, though, there was a little concern that she couldn't bring herself to address. Jillian wondered how a move like this would affect their financial future as a couple. Retirement was something they hadn't talked a lot about, and when she worked at Westbrook, it seemed clear she'd have a solid income through to 65 if she wanted. Things were different now. And while she knew they were in fairly good shape financially and had saved responsibly for retirement, she didn't want to make assumptions. She knew they should talk about it. Look at some real numbers. But all that was something she didn't want to deal with head-on yet. Anyway, if she didn't try to turn Sojourner around, she'd be out of a job immediately and back to the dismal prospect of perhaps never finding work again. At least with the current plan, it was feasible that she'd be back on salary with Sojourner just as quickly as they could raise a round. Well, that conversation could wait at least a couple days.

She smiled at Scott. "Amazing pork, Chef Johnson."

Monday morning as she swayed with the train, gripping tightly to the pole above her for balance, a voice played on repeat in Jillian's head like a self-improvement tape. *I will be a rational leader. I will temper my passion with good sense. I will exhibit wise skepticism.* Scott's initial caution was not lost on her. For now, she would let Rob be their gut check. He would have a handle on the financial side of things. And *he* certainly would not let himself be fooled twice.

By the time Jillian swiped her key card and pushed through the WeWork turnstiles, she was convinced. As the elevator reached the 12th floor, she was solid. When she pulled open the glass door with the large Sojourner logo, she was resolute. They should go for it.

All heads turned towards the door, silently acknowledging her entry. This was something new since Desmond died. Jillian always thought it odd that people could be so absorbed in work that they would not even look up when someone entered the room. Now, with Desmond's death they were orphans bound together for survival, which they signaled to each other even if without words. In any case, it was a welcome change to Jillian just to see their glances and head-nods, and she met their smiles with enthusiasm. And bagels.

"Happy Monday, guys. Carbs for all." She put the bag from Noah's Bagels on what used to be Desmond's desk. For a second that felt wrong, but only for a second. A muffled moan of gratitude ran through the room as she dropped her bag under her desk and took off her coat. She would miss this crew and the looming prospect of their disbandment intensified that. Funny how Rob had given the okay to work from home, but at a time like this they somehow were drawn instead to being together.

It was strange to fade from a job rather than to sprint towards an ending full-speed, such as one does when resigning with two weeks' notice, scrambling to finish up open projects before heading to a new employer. Instead, she and the whole Sojourner team would be slowly disappearing, like the trick ink Christian had loved to use as a kid.

Ten minutes before Trevor's meeting about Sojourner's resurrection, she closed up the document she was working on. She wanted some time to collect her thoughts before the meeting, maybe even coach herself to bring strong energy into the room. "Trevor, see you in Conference Room B in a few?" she whispered as she walked to the door. He nodded without looking away from his screen.

All the phone booths were full. She cursed WeWork under her breath and headed to the women's room, the only place one could find a little quiet. Space was tight in the restroom—not a square foot had been wasted. So she stood back-against-the-wall, her shoulder rubbing the hand dryer, as she silently reviewed the pros and cons of the opportunity. A freshly filled coffee mug warmed her hands. When a pair of women entered deep in office talk, they nearly bumped her. Ridiculous how small that bathroom was. She retreated to the conference room, waited in the hall for the meeting before theirs to break, then entered to wait.

Before long Trevor came in, almost giddy.

"So....," he began, his broad smile looking almost mischievous, as he pulled out a chair.

"So...., yourself. Let's get down to business." Somehow she meant it to come off friendlier, but Trevor didn't give her room to start again.

"You've got your serious face on, Jillian. Sounds like you want to make the case for resurrection."

"Impressive. You totally read that right. I didn't mean to be so obvious about it. Couldn't my so-called serious face mean a veto?"

"Telepathy, it's a mind-trick rarely used," he said, straightening up. "Anyway, I don't necessarily disagree, but I can see both sides. Why don't you outline why you think that's a good idea."

She went to the whiteboard and divided it in two with a broad stroke of the green marker. A classic pros/cons list. She'd already done that in her home office with Scott. She scribbled five bullet points under *Pros*. Taking a moment to step back and review, she then added a star with a flourish on one: *Build something we believe in.* Finally, she added a single *Con*, oversized and with several stars: *Unproven leadership—Would we invest in us?*

Trevor pulled on his chin, an invisible goatee. "I'm with you on it all. And the unproven leadership point is a strong one. It could outweigh all the pros, in fact. But you could also say we are proven—Rob, for one, knows we're straight shooters at least. I'd add one more con, too. *History.* Sojourner could be seen as damaged goods to investors and partners, even if we're not the ones responsible."

She added *History* to the right side, took a step back to survey, then added: *Can we book enough events to scale the program?* "It's always concerned me," she said, "that the more hotel partners we sign on, the more travelers and nonprofits we need to add, to keep the hotels happy. All sides of the marketplace need to be in lockstep to scale."

Jillian sat back down and they both pondered the whiteboard before them. The two columns were about even, a reality that disappointed slightly and kept them silent.

"Maybe we just need Rob to weigh in," Trevor said, finally. "After all, he's an actual investor and he knows what he bet on with Desmond. How about if we see if we can get him on the phone?"

There was no harm in trying, she thought as she texted Rob. Still, it was unlikely they could catch him at a gap in his schedule.

Rob immediately responded: "Sure, give me a call."

"It's our lucky day," she said with raised eyebrows, as she put her iPhone on the table and touched the screen to dial him. "Rob? Thanks for taking the call. I'm here with Trevor and you're on speaker." She and Trevor exchanged apprehensive glances. "We have a crazy idea for you," she said.

For the next ten minutes, the pair described their vision for taking over Sojourner, with all the positives and all the risks. Finally, Jillian came to the punctuation point: "Do you think we could raise funding?"

There was a silence on the other end. "Interesting proposition," Rob finally said. "But there's a lot you don't know yet about the business and where it sits today. Let me tell you that first."

A thorough review of the financials had yielded a truth both disturbing and hopeful, according to Rob. "As we guessed, payroll was out of whack. The forensic accountant has discovered that Desmond hired a hacker in Ukraine for a project it appears he was running on the side. We're not sure why yet, but it may have been out of desperation for raising some cash."

"For Sojourner?" Trevor asked.

"I don't think so. He and Anna were under the weight of some looming personal debt. I assume having the Pacific Heights and Lake Tahoe homes—easily two million dollars each—meant they were heavily mortgaged. And it sounds like they lived the high life. There's a lot more investigation that needs to be done. In any case, Desmond was paying this developer from Sojourner's wallet."

Jillian and Trevor exchanged puzzled glances. "What was the project?" she asked.

"That's where it gets really dicey. It would appear at this point—and they're still very early in the investigation—that the developer was hired to hack into hotel guest data through the API that Sojourner has access to. Desmond planned to sell that data on the dark web."

Trevor cursed. Jillian was silent, stunned.

"So Sojourner has been the conduit for hacking into the hotels?" Jillian couldn't help but think about how the hotels—her partners—were going to react when they learned this.

"Well yes, but it had nothing to do with the security on Sojourner's software. One could say the fault was in the back-office platform most hotels use, it had a vulnerability. That was quietly fixed earlier this week when it came to light. The hotels involved are intentionally keeping this quiet. Their security people aren't even telling their other departments."

Jillian breathed a sigh of relief. The new Sojourner would need these hotels as partners, and they'd need to see Sojourner as trusted.

"How many users and their data were affected?" Trevor asked.

"I guess the good news is that the intent was there, but they hadn't quite finished up the project to extract the data. It would appear that Desmond owed additional funds to the hacker, who was then threatening to go public with the project unless Desmond paid in full. The revenue he could get in the data sale would pay the hacker and ultimately his debt, but the timing kicked him. Desmond didn't count on having to pay the hacker in advance."

"Thus backing him into a very dark corner that he could not see his way out from," said Trevor.

"Exactly."

This was a lot to take in. "It's strange; I'm shocked but not," Jillian finally said. "In some ways, it explains a lot. Scott and I socialized once with Anna and Desmond, and it's not totally surprising that they were living above their means. But I never would have suspected anything criminal happening."

"I know this is tough news to process, and I'll send a detailed email to the entire staff once we hang up the phone. But I should circle back to my original assessment about the company's viability in the future. If one were to remove this fraud from the picture, which was motivated by something fully outside the realm of Sojourner, the company otherwise appears to be financially sound."

That was, of course, good news for Jillian and Trevor. It meant that at its core, something was working.

"Taking investment to the side as well as this hacker project, what do you think about Sojourner continuing as a viable business? Or better put, not *continuing* but being *reinvented*?" Trevor asked.

When Rob didn't jump to a response, Jillian rushed to preempt his answer, almost apologetically. "Well, it *was* a crazy idea. And maybe Trevor and I were just holding onto the dream. That we haven't moved past the denial stage to mourn Sojourner's demise."

"Don't be too hasty to judge my thoughts," Rob said. "Actually, I was just thinking that it makes sense. It'll be tough, but maybe you can raise a convertible note with a number of angel investors. Of course, it goes without saying that full transparency would be a cornerstone of the deal."

"So it's not a no?" she said, winking at Trevor.

"Two negatives don't necessarily make a positive in this case. But I'm open to exploring the idea. Why don't you put together a pitch for me and come in and do your thing. Then we'll see if it's worth bringing the pitch to other investors."

They agreed on a time to do so on Friday, and after they said their goodbyes Jillian and Trevor stared at each other with broad smiles. Terrified smiles.

"It's cliché, but, *Be careful what you wish for*," he said with air quotes. "Shit. Now we actually have to step up and do this. As if we know how."

"We can't let the world know what amateurs we are." She meant it as a joke, but there was truth in it.

They would have four days to create—or recreate—a solid business plan, map out the selling points in their pitch, then set it up in a beautifully designed deck. For a moment they considered using Desmond's, or some version of it, but then quickly decided against that. The situation called for a totally fresh start.

"We can do this," she said to Trevor. It was a phrase she and Scott used for each other, always with dramatic effect, whenever they had to do something they felt ill-equipped for. "We can do this," she repeated. "Now, we just need to tell the team, see who's in and who wants to move on, and then get to work. If we get a funding commitment quickly, we could salvage some of the team."

They wasted no time summoning an impromptu meeting in the middle of the office when they walked back in. Though Rob had said he would send an email detailing what Desmond had done, Jillian and Trevor couldn't keep the secret, recounting everything they had learned to their stunned coworkers. The reaction was intense, a mashup of disbelief and anger, and they sat talking about the situation for quite a while.

Finally, Jillian and Trevor announced their plan to resurrect Sojourner. Looking around the room, they posed the question: who's in?

Kaden already had a job lined up, but Alex and Nate seemed excited about the prospect. Jillian invited them all, even Kaden, to help create the pitch.

"So would you two be the co-founders?" Kaden asked, safe

territory for a short-timer.

Jillian looked at Trevor. She hadn't thought of it in those terms. It was logical, but there were repercussions to that.

"It's not anything we've even talked about," she said. "Or even thought about. I never wanted to be a founder, I just wanted to do something positive in the world. But I guess if that's what it takes…."

Trevor jumped in. "I always wanted to be a founder. I *wanted* the responsibility to run a company—and to do it right."

Jillian laughed. "We're clearly opposites. But for this co-founder business, let's just use one of my favorite phrases as a parent: 'We'll see.'"

Trevor stood up. "What pairs well with bagels? Well, don't even try to guess. It's champagne."

Jillian looked at the wall clock. Noon.

Trevor shrugged his shoulders playfully. "Well, as my dad liked to say, it's 5 o'clock somewhere…. Desmond stashed a bottle to celebrate when we eventually locked down the next round of funding. I think it's perfectly appropriate to crack it open now, without him." Trevor left the room to unearth the bottle from the large public refrigerator in the floor's kitchen, which otherwise housed a perpetual rotation of sack lunches, beverages, and Tupperware containers.

Meanwhile, Jillian dug through the only file cabinet in the office to look for the paper cups. She found the half-used package and set it down next to the bagels. "Over the Hill," the cups read. Apparently, someone had thought the irony funny for one of the 20-somethings' birthdays. She chuckled. For this occasion, they were just starting *up* the hill.

CHAPTER 26

E ven before Jillian pushed her weight against the door to enter Hog Island Oysters, she spotted Christian through the wall of windows, already at the table and scanning his phone. A rush of maternal pride washed over her. She had raised a little boy, who was suddenly a handsome, competent man.

Christian looked up and saw her enter, acknowledging her with a smile. She tossed the host a I-see-my-party-seated-already nod as she scurried by the cluster of people waiting for a table.

Seated and settled, Jillian couldn't help but say, "Have I mentioned lately how proud I am of you?"

"Yes, Mother, you say it all the time. But thank you." His smile seemed real. She knew he wouldn't *really* understand what she meant until he was a parent. And that would be a while.

They talked about everything parents and adult children do: his job, a new romantic interest, whether to renew the lease on his apartment, his grandfather's dementia. Finally, the conversation twisted toward her work.

"I don't think we've spoken since you went to Desmond's

funeral," he said, "and I was headed to London then so haven't heard the full scoop. Business travel sucks—especially out of the country. You get totally out of touch. So, what is the prognosis for Sojourner?" Christian scanned the menu as he asked, which struck Jillian as a little rude but not fully insulting coming from family. Plus she knew the server would be pressing them shortly, striving to turn the table quickly during the early evening rush. She picked up the menu and decided on the first viable option she saw: Cobb Salad. The server immediately appeared and took their order with extraordinary efficiency. Christian added a plate of oysters to share.

"Well, there's a crazy idea afoot now," she said, "and I need your professional input, a sound mind to double-check my thinking, to be sure I'm not jumping from the pan into the flame."

"Okay, you have my attention," he said with a curious smile that reminded her of when he'd get a clue about a Christmas gift but couldn't quite figure it out. Scott had loved to float impossible clues, crafted perfectly to taunt Christian.

He tore and dipped a piece of bread in olive oil as Jillian relayed what Rob told them about Desmond's improprieties, how otherwise the company was found to be financially solid, and that she and Trevor had earlier that day made an informal pitch to Rob Lockie for funding a new version of Sojourner, and he was interested enough to suggest a more formal pitch meeting. She narrated the tale of Sojourner's fall and possible rise again like a novel with plot twists and a complex cast of characters, while Christian followed the story arc with bead-like focus. He pursed his lips.

"So, you have just been ordained as a Sojourner advisor," she said. "First, what are your thoughts, as someone who knows the company's history, has experience with startups, and is a possible investor?"

"Well, let's not jump too far ahead. Remember that Pier 45 passed on Desmond's pitch."

"Oh, I'm not asking for funding from Pier 45. Really, I am not; that was a joke. But if I were, isn't it true that VCs generally base their bets on the team? That they invest based on confidence in the founders, even more than the product? I imagine that's important to you, too."

"Hmmm. I see I've been backed into a corner where my only choice is to express full confidence in my mother, or…"

"Exactly. If you want to get invited to Christmas dinner next year, you'll need to invest." She left just enough silence for it to be funny. "I'm kidding, of course. I have absolutely no expectation of funding from Pier 45. Anyway, I imagine you have some kind of policy to prevent friends and family investment. But I do expect your honest input on whether the team and I can do this. Even if it means you have to talk me out of it because you don't have confidence in *me*."

Christian thought for a minute. "I'd have to see the financials and get more information on any negligence on Desmond's part and how that impacted the bottom line."

"Actually, there's a lot more to tell you about Desmond." She went on to detail what Rob had revealed to her and Trevor the day before, that Showtime-series-worthy drama of disregard for the law, reckless behavior for the company, and ultimately, the darkest despair. As she did, she watched Christian's eyebrows raise. His usually relaxed face was drawn tight.

Jillian felt almost guilty to have been an unsuspecting bystander to Desmond's ill deeds. "I know, it's crazy and terrible. To think that was happening right under our noses. And what it drove Desmond to do. But all that aside, Rob says he thinks the company would be fine financially if Desmond weren't funneling funds away from the bottom line."

Christian put his hand out towards her to stop speaking, signaling that he needed a moment to process what she just told him. Finally, he collected himself. "As you say, that's crazy stuff. So maybe with that out of the picture, you have a shooting chance. Rob Lockie has a good reputation, so I would trust his judgment. But if you fail, and statistically that's likely—nothing personal—it'll be extremely painful because you'll have so much emotional ownership as a founder."

She nodded. She could tell it was already true. "Do you think we'll have trouble getting funding?"

"Tough call. I mean, Desmond wasn't having an easy time of it, but was that because of him or was it because of the company? If it's the latter, or both, you'll have trouble."

"How can I get feedback from VCs who rejected us?"

"VCs are notorious for not giving direct feedback. And who can blame us? It's awkward to deliver bad news, and we're all super busy. So you say, 'Call us when you're ready for your next round and we may be interested then.' It's the grownup version of ending a date with 'I'll call you.'"

Christian recommended setting up meetings with the funds that had rejected Desmond. That could capture any VCs who were passing on Sojourner based on lack of faith in the founder. "That's low-hanging fruit and you have nothing to lose," he said.

He suggested next researching funds and angel investors that had shown interest in social entrepreneurship with their investments. It was better than shooting in the dark, he said.

"Oh God, I have no experience pitching to VCs and neither does Trevor. Pitching could be a disaster." Scott and Christian were the only two humans on the planet she could say this to. Even saying it out loud made her nervous. Would that make it real?

"You should give yourself more credit. You have tons of experience convincing large organizations to hold their big-budget events in your hotel. And you have a keen sense of logic and design in the way you talk to people. Layer that with a humility that comes off as very authentic, and you are miles ahead of many founders. And certainly Desmond."

"If you thought he was a loser, then why did you refer me to the job?"

He laughed. "I didn't really say he was a loser. Although I guess it turned out that he was. Anyway, the concept of Sojourner is such a perfect fit for you, that I chose to disregard Desmond's deficits. And look how nicely it worked out!"

"Nicely? Desmond killed himself after trying to steal data from our customers and sell it on the dark web. Not exactly a fairy tale ending." Her tilted head showed a kind of nonverbal *gotcha*.

"Yup, you got me there." He winked. "So anyway, I can help you with the pitch. It's straightforward what you need to do, and you can keep it brief. Describe the problem, then describe how the product solves it. Tell how you make money. Detail how much you made last month and how much you're projected to make this year. Be upfront about what happened to the old Sojourner and why the new company is different. Fill in the cracks between with anything else that feels good. But be sure you're truthful. It saves time."

Jillian left the restaurant buoyed. With two strong VC allies in Christian and Rob, she began to actually believe she and Trevor could give Sojourner new life and get funding.

An hour later when she walked in the front door at home, the voices of Jennifer Aniston and David Schwimmer wafted from the den. Scott was streaming *Friends*, and she followed the sound down the hall like a dog to an unattended meal. Jillian loved the cozy warren of their Craftsman house, so counter to the current trend of wide-open interiors. The den's chocolate brown walls, which were lined with built-in bookcases and painted a crisp white, fully stocked with their reading history, made it a refuge from the chaos of life. She threw off her coat and shoes and plopped down in the leather chair.

"What's the news from the startup trenches?" Scott asked, clicking *Pause* on the remote as she plopped, before she had a chance to ask him to. That request was her habit, and in the last couple years he had learned to preempt it.

"We're so lucky to have a son who's turned out so well. In spite of us."

"This is not news, but yes. What did Christian think of your vision for Sojourner?"

"I'd call it *guarded optimism*. He warned of the potential problems and the possibility of failure, which I suppose is good advice, but he was also very encouraging."

Scott grinned. "Your voice sounds confident, like you're ready to do this. And that's perfect. Half the battle is emotional. Maintaining the confidence level and having the grit to wade through some tough times."

"You read that right. Per usual. Even so, I'm tired and am going to get ready for bed. Feel free to continue as you were, in case you want to finish Season 20 or something tonight."

"For the record, there are only eight seasons of *Friends*. I'll finish up the episode and see you upstairs."

She gave him a Rob-and-Laura-Petrie peck and trudged up the stairs to the master bedroom, which occupied the entire second floor. Though tempted to throw herself onto the bed for a momentary rest, she knew it would be a disaster—she'd fall asleep with her clothes on. Instead, she went straight to the bathroom to wash her face. Leaning into the oversized vanity mirror, she examined her face. Somehow, all she could see was the sagging skin around her mouth and wrinkles on her neck. The title of Nora Ephron's classic essay, "I Feel Bad About My Neck," came to mind. This was not the neck of a startup founder. But she was too tired to obsess further about aging and simply washed her face.

Jillian grabbed her pajamas from the hook in her closet and hastily changed, leaving a pile of clothes draped over the back of the wingback chair in a corner of the bedroom. When she purchased the chair years ago during a random stroll through Macy's, she envisioned a reading nook where she'd curl up with a book. Instead, it had mainly become a convenient receptacle for stashing clothes when she was too tired to hang them up.

She crawled into bed, turned off the light, and didn't even think about grabbing a book to read. *I'm going to need a solid eight hours of sleep if I'm going to compete with the cool kids.* This was her last thought until she awoke, glanced at the alarm clock, sighed at 3:14 blazing in red light, and began her nightly meditations to coax herself back to sleep.

CHAPTER 27

Less than 24 hours later, the shit hit the fan with her parents. Or that's how Jillian looked at it, when the shock of reality cut through her fantasy perspective. These things always started with a phone call. Given the events of the last month, Jillian found herself tense up when the phone rang.

Her mother. She picked up.

The call shifted quickly from the exchange of hellos. "Honey, I wanted your father to talk to you, and I'm going to put him on the phone."

"Of course, I'd love to talk with him."

"The thing is, he's a bit confused this morning. I don't know how to explain it. Disoriented maybe. Anyway, I thought hearing your voice would reset him. Somehow."

It was starting. She took a breath. "Oh Mom, this must be really hard for you. Put him on the line and let's see if it helps."

Jillian could hear her mother handing the phone to her father. "Jillian's on the phone, Thomas. She wanted to talk to you. Jillian, our daughter."

Jillian tensed up, unsure what she would say to her own father. And worse, what he might say.

"Hi Dad, it's me. Jillian. How are you doing today?"

"Fine thank you."

She couldn't read whether the stiffness was because he didn't recognize her and was being polite to a stranger. Or maybe he did recognize her voice and was still being polite? Either way, there was no choice but to forge ahead.

"How's the weather out by you guys? Do you have any snow left on the ground?" Safe bet, weather. Concrete. She imagined him looking out the kitchen window at their yard, to make the determination.

He reported there was no snow.

"All melted, huh?" she said, relaxing a little. "We had rain last night, so more snow may be headed your way. I'm guessing it'll turn to snow at your elevation. Hey, I've been wanting to tell you about something big at work." Just as she said this, she remembered that she purposely had not told her parents about leaving Westbrook. At the time, she feared they would be stressed by her leap. And now…well, the potential stress was greater. Exponentially. *Hey Mom and Dad, I meant to tell you: I left my secure job for an early-stage startup, and then my new boss killed himself, his wife is being investigated for fraud, and now the company is declaring bankruptcy. But don't worry: I plan to take the dead-company-with-a-cloud-of-fraud-over-it, and turn it into a unicorn. And again, not to worry, I'm not doing it alone: I have a 23-year-old co-founder.*

"Really, what's happened at Westbrook?" he asked.

The specificity of her father's question jolted her. He remembered she worked at Westbrook? She was suspended mid-air between a jump of relief at his recall and a dive of shame at being trapped in the lie she was about to tell.

"Oh, well," she said, stalling, trying to come up with a believable lie. "Well, I won the Sales Executive of the Year Award," she said. It was for his own good, she told herself.

"That's just wonderful honey. I'll tell your mother. Once we get home."

"I thought you *were* home. Where are you calling from?"

There was no response. And her mother got on the phone, having been passed the handset.

"Jillian? Just a minute while I step into the bedroom." Jillian heard a door close.

"Mom, that was weird. You're at home, right?"

"Well, he got confused again at the end, but it was great that he recognized your voice and could ask about Westbrook. What's happened at work?"

"Oh, it's nothing really. But how could he not even recognize that he's home?" This made no sense to Jillian. She thought perhaps she had misread her father's meaning.

"It happens from time to time. I'm just trying to stay positive. To roll with it. And to be sure he takes the medication daily."

Her mother was a saint. Solid like the concrete foundation on a home. She hoped she could learn to be half the woman her mother was. Living with Alzheimer's was a harder task than resuscitating a company, and for a moment she felt shame in feeling so stressed over Sojourner.

Should she tell her mother about Sojourner, even though she didn't want her father to know? She was dying for her mother's unwavering vote of confidence about the work, but that was selfish. She could survive without it, because it would unfair to add another worry to her mother's burden.

"Well like you said, Mom, I'm glad my voice connected with him, and hopefully it'll help keep him settled today. Be sure to call me whenever you want, Mom. And maybe I can drive up in the next couple weeks. Take you guys out for lunch. Maybe even spend the night."

"That would be lovely. But we know you have a lot going on. Give our love to Scott and Christian. I want to get back out to the kitchen to make sure your dad's okay."

Crap, Jillian thought as she put the phone down on the kitchen counter. When you read about the "Sandwich Generation" it usually meant being squeezed between taking care of children and aging parents. In her case, she was squeezed between an adolescent company and Alzheimer's. *It sucks to be me*, she thought. Just then Scott came into the kitchen, coffee mug in hand and grinning. She felt ashamed of her self-pity, returned the smile, and pulled herself together.

She had barely refilled her coffee when her phone rang again. Trevor. She was actually relieved to see his name, not her mother's. She couldn't explain the relief, because Sojourner and whatever was on Trevor's mind demanded more of her resources. Counted totally on her. But her ties to her parents were so deep and lifelong. It was beneath all that mattered to her. And the instability of her father's cognitive state was totally unsettling. She was starting to realize how much of her own identity was anchored in her vision of her parents as intelligent, capable, and independent. These qualities in them corresponded to the same qualities in herself. She saw herself as their creation. And now a crack had opened, destabilizing her. But enough. She would need to come back to that. For now, she put it aside to reclaim her Sojourner identity.

"Wow. It must be a national emergency to have merited an actual phone call," she said to Trevor, without waiting for a greeting. She meant this strictly as a joke, because the Sojourner employees were completely phone-averse. But whatever had escalated to phone call level put her on alert.

"I'm just lazy, honestly," Trevor said. "I wanted to ask you a few things and couldn't bear typing them out."

Her shoulders relaxed slightly. "I get it, believe me. You can cover so much more ground in a single phone call. Congratulations on being the very first person in your generation to learn this. So what's up?"

"I actually have a list of things."

She smiled. Very Trevor.

"First up, Jillian, we need to get the pitch deck finalized. Are you coming into the office today?"

"Yes, after lunch. We can work heads down on it then. Next on the list?"

"Financial stuff." There were so many financial issues they would need to resolve, bills to pay. He also suggested they plan a phone call with a consultant he found who specialized in emerging from bankruptcy. "We've got one shot to do this, so we need to be really smart about it."

Of course, he was right, and it was something she hadn't thought of. Was she surprised because of his age? Or some preconceived notion she had about developers' intelligence limited to coding? Or the judgments she had made about his lifestyle? She'd need to give her biases another look. When she turned 50, she'd vowed to give up judgment. To be fair, at the time she had not realized how judgment infused so many of her thoughts. A fair-minded liberal, she'd considered herself as nonjudgmental as any of her friends. So wrong, so wrong. Nonjudgment would be a decades-long project.

When Jillian hung up, she put a meeting with Trevor on the calendar for later in the day. She looked over at the sunlight streaming through the window in the kitchen nook. She would treat herself to five minutes of quiet reflection sitting at the table with a cup of tea. She would not think about work. She would not think about her parents. She would just enjoy the warmth of the sun on this otherwise brisk day. Just enjoy it. Then, and only then, would she face reality.

CHAPTER 28

Several days later, Jillian hurried down Market Street, glancing at the time. She'd left work early to stop in at Braverman's Luggage & More and they closed at 5. Scott's birthday was coming up, and he'd commented on a suitcase several months earlier as he scrolled through a *Travel + Leisure* article—a luggage brand she'd never heard of called Nonstop. Scott rarely cared about anything that could be considered chic, so she made a mental note to check out this shiny, hard-sided bag. It made her chuckle to think about it, really, because the bag was so bling-y, so not Scott. She wanted to take a close look, to get a feel for whether he'd actually like it in real life.

Trevor had also left work early to beat traffic to a concert he was going to that evening in the South Bay. As if it were possible to beat traffic at any hour in the Bay Area lately. It was a well deserved early exit for both: they made good headway on their pitch deck that day. As she walked, she mused that not having a CEO gave her a sense of freedom—such as to leave whenever she wanted—which she technically had with Desmond but never felt like she did. She suspected Trevor sensed it, too.

As she walked towards the luggage store, Jillian passed Alex & Andrew's, San Francisco's coolest independent bookstore, and without planning to, turned around and ducked in. She was curious about a book on pitching mentioned in a podcast—the book was supposed to be amazing—and she wanted to leaf through it. But the Barnes & Noble near her house had closed. Surely they'd have it at Alex & Andrew's. Once through the door, it took only a moment to find the business section, and the book was prominently displayed there, a staff pick. *You know you're in San Francisco when a pitch book is a staff pick*, she thought. She thumbed through, stopping every few pages to read. Pretty insightful. She and Trevor could go through it tomorrow to do a final upgrade to their deck.

Fumbling through her purse as she walked to the cashiers, Jillian then looked up and there she was—Anna, her back to Jillian and right ahead of her in line. Jillian recognized the jet-black bob immediately, even from the back. Yet Anna looked like she'd been tumble dried and tried to put herself back together again. This was awkward. Perhaps she could quickly walk back to the business section and wait until Anna left the store. Which is when Anna happened to turn and her eyes met Jillian's.

"Oh, Anna, hello," Jillian said, trying to sound natural. "Hard to resist a physical bookstore these days, huh?" She paused and then considered Anna's situation. "How are you *doing?*" she said, trying to sound compassionate but not syrupy. *Consider the widow, not the fraud.*

Anna looked momentarily like a trapped animal, eyes quickly leaving Jillian's, but she composed herself in a split second. "It's a tough time, in just about every way. Thanks for asking. I know things have been hard at Sojourner, too."

It was ironic to hear Anna say this, since she presumably had been an accomplice in the lifestyle that had been the impetus of much of this hardship, but Jillian resisted the urge to respond. She saw the stack of books in Anna's arms: *The Subtle Art of Not Giving a F*ck*, *Resilience*, and a novel emblazoned with a *Best Beach Reading by O*

Magazine sticker. We are what we read.

"Listen, Jillian. Would you mind having a cup of coffee with me? It would really help me to talk with you."

This was the last thing Jillian expected to hear, and the last thing she wanted. But her sense of decency wouldn't allow her to say no. "Sure. I can meet you in the store cafe after we pay." She wanted to get it over with. To have put something on the calendar would allow dread to grow by the hour. One of the cashiers beckoned Anna with an I-can-help-the-next-person-in-line wave, and Jillian was immediately called by another cashier.

Having just one book, Jillian finished checking out first. Anna was arguing with the cashier about a price, and Jillian nodded to her as she passed by and headed upstairs to the cafe. She ordered a decaf Americano, not wanting to risk even the small amount of caffeine in her preferred green tea, and sat down at a table set off to the side, trying to hide her nerves by checking email. She didn't want Anna to see her book, making sure it was carefully concealed in her tote. What could Anna possibly want?

When Anna appeared at the top of the escalator, she didn't bother ordering and instead approached Jillian's table directly, putting her bag on the floor, and sat with a flourish like an exclamation mark at the end of a sentence.

"This is hard for me, but I want to do it. I need to apologize to you and to everyone at Sojourner. I'm sure you know by now that Desmond siphoned some cash from the company, and we can only speculate, but I'm sure that had a lot to do with his suicide. And I know that put you guys in a bad spot and the company is closing. But I wanted to tell you face-to-face that I'm sorry he did that."

Jillian did not know what to say. The only reason Anna was saying this was that they happened to bump into each other. And anyway, she was apologizing for Desmond, not her own role in the mess.

"Okay. Thanks, Anna. The thing is that we're doing just fine. We're actually planning to reorganize the company once the finances are straightened out."

Jillian felt regret the moment these words came from her mouth. Obviously, she wanted to hurt Anna by putting Desmond down. This was unkind, she knew.

Anna cast her eyes downward. "Good for you. I'm sure you'll do well." The statement fell flat, followed by silence.

"What's ahead for you?" Jillian asked. Jillian's question came out like asking about Anna's career, innocent-sounding—though it was not.

"Actually, fraud charges have been filed by the investors. So I'm left to deal with this, while Desmond very conveniently removed himself from responsibility. Honestly, I feel like it's small potatoes, compared to what the FBI usually deals with so it won't go anywhere. But in the meantime, I'm in limbo. My assets have been frozen. I still have my job, but that's tenuous. My parents are basically saving my butt, and I've been forced to move back in with them. Like a college kid. Not to mention that the love of my life is gone."

Jillian felt a flicker of sympathy but checked herself. Anna and Desmond's greed—or whatever had caused the fraud—had negatively affected all those in their path. She forced herself to remember that while Anna was feeling sorry for herself, Rob had lost a million dollars in investment, and the rest of them were out of jobs. Still, her higher self wanted the conversation to end on a generous note, even if that wasn't her presiding emotion. "I appreciate the apology, Anna. And I'll tell the others. I wish you the best. I really do." She stood and offered her hand to Anna.

Anna finally took the hand and shook without vigor. "Thanks for listening, Jillian. And all the best with Sojourner."

Jillian nodded and walked to the escalator, feeling Anna's eyes on her back. She thought again about the books Anna had purchased. Maybe she really did want to turn things around. For years Jillian had tried to assume positive intent with people she didn't trust. Today was a real test of her ability to do that. Anyway, there was a mountain of work to do and she couldn't afford to be distracted by manufactured feelings about Anna that may or may not be true.

Exiting the bookstore, plodding down the sidewalk, she refocused on the suitcase. In light of the conversation with Anna, the suitcase now seemed trivial. Then Jillian picked up her pace: actually, a gift for Scott was exactly what mattered.

The next day when she walked into the office, Jillian pulled out the book—*Pitch Academy*—and threw it down on Trevor's desk. "This is going to be our bible." He looked up at her, amused.

"If only…," was all he had to say and she knew what he meant. And agreed. They both knew they needed more help than a book, but they were going to take the guidance wherever they could get it.

"Hey, you would not believe who I had coffee with last night," Jillian blurted out.

Trevor's eyes squinted.

"Well, don't even try to guess. Anna. I ran into Anna when I was buying the book and she asked to have coffee with me. And apparently the purpose was to apologize."

One eyebrow moved up Trevor's forehead. "Apologize? You're fucking kidding me."

"It is kind of ridiculous, but I am trying to give her the benefit of the doubt. I think it's possible she was honestly trying to make amends."

"To what end?"

"What if forgiveness can help her move on? Bounce back?"

"What planet are you living on? I don't want her to bounce back. What about us? We're not exactly bouncing. We were slammed to the floor and are now clawing our way back, not bouncing."

Jillian sighed and nodded reluctantly. What she was thinking, though, was that it really didn't matter whether he assumed positive intent. What mattered was that she did, and that at the same time she did her best to give Trevor what he needed. "Anyway, we have work to do." Jillian hung up her coat, went to her desk, sat down, and flipped open her laptop.

They were cramming for their pitch to Rob the next day. Rob was a soft start, almost a dress rehearsal. And assuming that went well, they planned to next target a VC Desmond had claimed wanted in on the next round, Len Stillwater. Perhaps Stillwater would cut Trevor and Jillian a break because of Desmond's death. A sympathy meeting. No matter, they'd take what they could get.

"Let's do one more pass through the deck, then review it again in light of the book," she said to Trevor.

"In light of the book? You only this minute gave it to me."

"Don't worry. There's a summary in the back. We can just take each of the bullets and see if we hit the mark."

Trevor sighed. "You always have a plan, don't you?" The remark sounded critical, but he glanced over at Jillian and met her eyes, and allowed a slight smile to creep across his face.

CHAPTER 29

The irony of having a celebration on Sojourner's final payday was not lost on Jillian as she walked down the hall, a wine bottle in each hand. Their pitch with Rob had gone well, and he was already helping them work with the attorneys on the company's transition. In the meantime, he suggested they immediately start talking to other VCs. So they're managed to get a last-minute slot on Len Stillwater's calendar that morning and the pitch hadn't gone badly. It was too early to tell, and he said he'd get back to them, but at least they hadn't embarrassed themselves. Now, as the end of the day approached, they were ready to let it all go and mark the milestone—the last day of the old Sojourner.

Trevor and Alex had gone down to the lobby to retrieve the delivery of Chinese food and cupcakes. Jillian marveled that you could order delivery for just about anything these days in San Francisco. As she pushed open the glass door, Nate, who was on a chair taping up a web of green streamers, looked over. The streamers draped every which way from the ceiling, a wonderfully juvenile show of spirit. "Hey, I took leadership in high school. Which makes me an expert on putting up streamers," Nate said.

Earlier that day, Jillian had feared a party was in poor taste, but in the end she couldn't talk herself out of it. After all, despite hardships—including death and fraud—life goes on and so were the Sojourner employees. For Kaden, it was a time to hug, to say goodbye, and to hope future connection would not merely be on LinkedIn. For Alex and Nate, who would stay on, it was a lifeline. For Trevor and Jillian, it was a meaningful turning point. What they were going to create would be wholly their own, not just a continuation of what Desmond had built. Trevor would get to be a cofounder just as he'd always wanted, and Jillian would get to do good in a way she cared about. *Such a hopeful moment*, she thought as she walked.

A month ago they would have said Desmond built a valuable business, but really, he hadn't. It crumbled and so did he, the biggest fail of all. For Jillian, one of the most exciting things about the new Sojourner was that she could do things *her* way. With Trevor, of course. But the two of them had such complementary skills, and of course solid trust and communication, so this would feel very different from work for Desmond.

As she approached the office, Jillian was struck by how it had changed. Yes, today there were streamers. But beyond that, it just felt different. A lot of the clutter from the desks had been packed up, as had the rag-tag collection of logo-stamped marketing junk that had accumulated from conferences and salespeople over the previous year. The bookcase, which had long been a disorganized repository for an odd assortment of business books, was now ship-shape after Jillian tidied it one afternoon in a cyclone of activity. Funny how she felt a new emotional ownership of things as trivial as the bookcase.

She watched Nate step back down onto the floor from a skittery chair on wheels after taping the last piece of green crepe paper to the glass. Desmond's desk had been pushed into the center of the room and paired with the empty desk that generally served as a snack area. They would need to move everything Monday morning when the new-and-improved Sojourner downsized to a smaller office, but for today it was worth it to have the setting fit the mood.

Through the glass door, Jillian saw Trevor and Alex walking towards the office, chatting as if without a care, a bag in each hand. Then, as they arranged the take-out boxes on Desmond's old desk, the greasy smell of pot stickers permeated the room. Someone made a joke about partying, while Jillian twisted the tops off the wine bottles, and Nate put on some music. The remaining Over the Hill paper goods completed the buffet.

"Let's vow that this is the last celebration for these birthday items. Either we use every last cup and plate today, or we toss what remains," Trevor said. "And whoever wants beer, take one of these cups down to the kitchen to fill it. Don't you dare use the WeWork cups until we're out of Over the Hill!" Nate left the room, cup in hand.

Jillian thought about a fitting toast. Somehow it would fall to her to do it, but such things didn't come naturally. In social situations, Scott, the extrovert in the family, usually stepped forward when a toast was required. She'd done a quick search earlier on her phone for "toasts at work," didn't see anything appropriate in the results, and decided to just talk off the cuff. She could end up with a succinct, "To us," and that would have to do the job when the time came.

Everyone began filling their plates. It was a small enough group that they could sit around in a circle and have a single conversation.

"What are the craziest memories you have of Sojourner?" Jillian asked no one in particular. "I have the shortest tenure here, but I'm guessing some pretty over-the-top things have happened amongst you guys."

Alex told a story about when Nate brought his dog to work and it had not gone well. While Jillian thought it was somewhat amusing, the others rolled in laughter. Clearly you had to have been there.

Trevor reminisced about when they had all been locked out of the previous office and decided to go to a bar to work, but had instead gotten drunk as a group.

"I can see I came way too late to the game," Jillian said. This was her transition to the toast, and she held up her cup. She said some words about how impressed she was with the company and the team when she interviewed, and that her time as an employee had only boosted that. They'd been through a lot together, the good and the bad, and it made her happy to know everyone was starting an exciting new chapter. "To us! Definitely not Over the Hill. Yet."

Rather than clinking, their paper cups made no sound as they bumped.

As they finished up the shrimp fried rice and sweet and sour chicken—the pot stickers had been snatched up immediately—Jillian felt the glow of a relaxed, comfortable companionship. She had feared starting Sojourner again from scratch, that it would be hard to build a healthy company culture. But maybe they were halfway there already. Nothing like trauma to bond you.

She cut through the tab of scotch tape with her nail to open up the cupcake box.

"No birthday candles needed for these, guys. Sugar up!" she said, licking chocolate frosting from her fingertips.

After they said emotional goodbyes, Jillian and Trevor shushed everyone out. She said, "Leave the cleanup to us. We're going to need to do some humility training before the co-founder titles go to our heads."

But as she busied herself wiping down Desmond's desk with a wet paper towel, she felt a sudden panic. Was she crazy to be "founding" a startup? Even if the company already existed—which made it more of a re-start? Who was she kidding to think she could run a company?

Trevor was busy at the garbage can separating recycling from the rest. Somehow, that reassured her. He was a conscientious partner. The door slid open behind her.

"Did I miss the party? Is it too late to break out the whiskey?" Christian held out a bottle of Jack Daniels like a dumbbell. "Whiskey is a must-have for launching a business."

She dropped the boxes hastily into the trash can and turned to hug him. "Too late? Never. For you. And booze." Jillian introduced Christian to Trevor, who was clearly amused.

"Hey Trevor," she said, "isn't this just perfect? Because we happen to have these Over the Hill paper cups we were going to have to throw away…." She grabbed the last three and set them out on the table. "Christian, take off your coat, open the bottle and do the honors of pouring, please. Fair warning, we've had some wine already."

Christian's eyes went to the recycling bin and eyed the two bottles, eyebrows raised. Jillian noticed. "Right, well, one was open already, and there *were* three other people here," she said, feeling like he was the parent, not her.

"No worries. We'll let Uber and BART drive us home," he said.

Christian made the toast, and the three sat lazily around the desks in the center of the room, chatting about fundraising.

"Jillian told me you were a VC," Trevor said, "and that she'd gotten the lead on the job because you'd met Desmond, but I had no appreciation for just how helpful you can be to us going forward—and probably already have been. Jillian, why were you holding out on me and keeping our secret weapon, secret?"

"I guess I wanted to do it on my own. I wanted to figure out how to make it work without leaning too heavily on Christian."

"My God, Mom. You sound like I did when I didn't want any help on my college essay."

"The analogy doesn't make sense. Parents are there to help their children."

"And adult children are not there to help their parents?"

"Listen, give me 40 years and yes, I'll be happy to accept help moving into the nursing home. When I don't know which way is up and who you are. I guess I don't want to withdraw from the goodwill bank account too soon."

"Speaking of bank accounts…," Trevor said.

The three of them laughed at the transition and talked about the plans to give Sojourner enough runway to revive itself.

Jillian looked at her watch. "Trevor, what do you say we close the proverbial door on this iteration of Sojourner? I can meet you here at 9 a.m. sharp on Monday, when we have the elevator reserved. Luckily, we're only going eight floors. But it might as well be eight miles for all the work it'll be for four people."

"Except that at eight miles, we'd need to deal with rain and traffic."

"Always one to see the positive, Trevor," Jillian said.

"Have you forgotten our first conversation, when I suspected that something was awry with our company finances? Not exactly an optimist."

"Well, when it's fact, the glass is neither half-full nor half empty. It just is."

"I'm not sure that makes sense, Mom."

"Whose side are you on, anyway? Trevor is the logical one in this partnership anyway."

They moved into the hallway, slid the glass door behind them, and locked up. Jillian touched the Sojourner logo lightly, like a mother blessing her child on the cheek. "See you Monday, Sojourner."

THE END

Book Club Discussion Questions

The themes in *Employee 6 Is 54* can spark great conversations about the intersection of age and work. Members of your book club can dig into their own experiences in the workplace and the tensions of being "older" in the workforce. It's an especially interesting conversation when the group is intergenerational.

1. Jillian thought little about re-employment before quitting her hotel job. But once she started looking and was having no response, she began to think of herself as being too old and too expensive. What hurdles have you seen for older people in job search? What advice would you give someone looking for a new job at 56?

2. Jillian's husband, Scott, is very supportive when she quit her job without another lined up. Is this realistic? What has been your experience with the tensions between spouses during a period of unemployment?

3. Even highly experienced employees, when put in new situations (like Jillian was), can have their confidence undermined. How did Jillian respond to this, and what are some practical ways to boost confidence in a new workplace?

4. After she began working at Sojourners, Jillian noticed she had her own biases against the younger people on the team. For example, they came in late and they communicated primarily on Slack rather than face-to-face. What biases or "stories" have you noticed about different generations? Are they based in reality?

5. There is a lot of generational warring in the media, especially social media. Examples: Gen Zers telling millennials that skinny jeans and side parts are for old people; the "ok boomer" slam; and saying the laughing-while-crying emoji is a boomer giveaway. Have you noticed any of these zingers? Are these funny or harmful?

6. Jillian's husband, Scott, was grooming a younger employee to take over the board shop business. Family businesses commonly employ multiple generations in the family. What are some dynamics you've noticed in how family businesses handle age differences, especially in succession plans? Scott and his protege seemed to have a happy working relationship. Do you have a sense of how they might have been able to achieve this?

7. Jillian's son, Christian, is an enormous help to her career, introducing her to Desmond, guiding her in how to pitch, and helping her understand Sojourner's financials. Have you ever gotten great advice or guidance from your child?

8. Jillian's parents are dealing with her father's dementia, and she wants to help yet is stressed with work and sadness about her father's diagnosis. How have you dealt with family caregiving tasks and the tensions surrounding these?

9. Priorities late in your career can differ from years earlier. How have you seen your career goals change over time? Are you a can't-wait-to-retire kind of person, or will-never-stop-working, or somewhere in between?

10. At early-stage startups, employees are generally paid below-market rates—to allow the company to conserve capital—while promising a larger payoff in stock ownership if the company is successful. Given that 50% of startups fail, is this a tradeoff you'd make?

11. What big lessons have you learned through work experience? What do you know now that you didn't when you first went to work?

Author's Note

Thanks so much for reading *Employee 6 Is 54*. If you enjoyed it, I'd very much appreciate a review on Amazon. Reviews like yours help other readers find this book.

I hope this book sparks your interest in the value that older employees bring to startups in particular, as well as the challenges they face (such as ageism). To stay abreast of these issues and what I'm writing on these topics, sign up at www.startupdecoder.com and receive my updates.

Acknowledgements

To my mind, one of the best aspects of working on a small team like that of Sojourner, is the people. I am extremely grateful for my former colleagues, who have accepted me, inspired me, and provided me with countless opportunities. Working at an early-stage startup is a wild ride by most standards, and I thrilled at the ups (and tried to stoically stomach the downs).

Many colleagues and friends have provided input on this book. I could not have done this without the help of Joanne Hartman, who from Day One encouraged me in writing and has patiently provided invaluable editing and input on this book. The talented Daniel Payne designed the cover. And special thanks to early readers Joanie Muench, Sandy Pruessner, and Janet Libert.

Most of all, there is Joe. An overly enthusiastic reader, patient partner, and endless cheerleader.

Nancy Branka is a writer, editor and founder of Startup Decoder, a website for mid- and late-career employees in startups and tech. Prior, she served for four years as chief content officer for Bizly, an early-stage startup, and 14 years as managing editor of *Executive Travel Magazine*, a Time Inc./American Express Publishing title. She lives in South Carolina with her husband and two sons.

*9 7 8 1 7 3 7 7 2 1 1 0 9 *